Double Duty for the Cowboy

Brenda Harlen

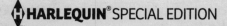

HARLEQUIN®SPECIAL EDITION

Recycling programs
for this product may
not exist in your area.

ISBN-13: 978-1-335-57385-8

Double Duty for the Cowboy

Copyright © 2019 by Brenda Harlen

Printed in U.S.A.

Brenda Harlen is a former attorney who once had the privilege of appearing before the Supreme Court of Canada. The practice of law taught her a lot about the world and reinforced her determination to become a writer—because in fiction, she could promise a happy ending! Now she is an award-winning, RITA® Award–nominated national bestselling author of more than thirty titles for Harlequin. You can keep up-to-date with Brenda on Facebook and Twitter or through her website, brendaharlen.com.

Books by Brenda Harlen

Harlequin Special Edition

Match Made in Haven

The Sheriff's Nine-Month Surprise
Her Seven-Day Fiancé
Six Weeks to Catch a Cowboy
Claiming the Cowboy's Heart

Those Engaging Garretts!

A Wife for One Year
The Daddy Wish
A Forever Kind of Family
The Bachelor Takes a Bride
Two Doctors & a Baby
Building the Perfect Daddy
Baby Talk & Wedding Bells
The Last Single Garrettt

Montana Mavericks: The Lonelyhearts Ranch

Bring Me a Maverick for Christmas!

Montana Mavericks: The Great Family Roundup

The Maverick's Midnight Proposal

Visit the Author Profile page
at Harlequin.com for more titles.

For my readers—because I would never have made it to this milestone book (#50) without you!

Prologue

It had been a fairly quiet week in Haven, and Connor Neal was grateful that trend seemed to be continuing on this Friday night of the last long weekend of summer. Sometimes the presence of law enforcement was enough to deter trouble, so the deputy had parked his patrol car in front of Diggers' Bar & Grill and strolled along Main Street.

There was a crowd gathered outside Mann's Theater, moviegoers waiting for the early show to let out so they could find their seats for the late viewing. Construction workers were sawing and hammering inside The Stagecoach Inn, preparing the old building for its grand reopening early in the New Year. Half a dozen vehicles were parked by The Trading Post; several people lingered over coffee and conversation at The Daily Grind.

He waved at Glenn Davis, as the owner of the hardware store locked up, then resumed his journey. Making his way back toward Diggers', he heard the unmistakable sound of retching. Apparently, patrol tonight was going to include chauffeur service for at least one inebriated resident, which was preferable to letting a drunk navigate the streets. He only hoped that whoever would be getting into the backseat of his car for the ride home had thoroughly emptied their stomach first.

He followed the sound around to the side of the building, where he discovered a nicely shaped derriere in a short navy skirt, beneath the hem of which stretched long, shapely legs. He felt a familiar tug low in his belly that immediately identified the owner of those sexy legs—it was the same reaction he had whenever he was in close proximity to Regan Channing.

She braced a hand on the brick and slowly straightened up, and he could see that she wore a tailored shirt in a lighter shade of blue with the skirt, and her long blond hair was tied back in a loose ponytail. She turned around then, and her eyes—an intriguing mix of green and gray—widened with surprise.

Her face was pale and drawn, her cheekbones sharply defined, her lips full and perfectly shaped. It didn't seem to matter that she'd been throwing up in the bushes, Regan Channing was still—to Connor's mind—the prettiest girl in all of Haven, Nevada.

She pulled a tissue out of her handbag and wiped her mouth.

He gave her a moment to compose herself before he said, "Are you okay?"

"No." She shook her head, those gorgeous eyes filling with tears. "But thanks for asking."

He waited a beat, but apparently she didn't intend to say anything more on the subject. He took the initiative again. "Can I give you a ride home?"

"No need," she said. "I've got my car."

"Maybe so, but I don't think you should be driving."

"I'm feeling a lot better now—really," she told him.

"I'm glad," he said. "But I can't let you get behind the wheel in your condition."

"My condition?" she echoed, visibly shaken by his remark. "How do you know—" she cut herself off, shaking her head again. "You don't know. You think I've been drinking."

"It's the usual reason for someone throwing up outside the town's favorite watering hole," he noted.

Regan nodded, acknowledging the validity of his point. "But I'm not drunk… I'm pregnant."

Chapter One

Six-and-a-half months later

Regan shifted carefully in the bed.

She felt as if every muscle in her body had been stretched and strained, but maybe that was normal after twenty-two hours of labor had finally resulted in the birth of her twin baby girls. Despite her aches, the new mom felt a smile tug at her lips when she looked at the bassinet beside her hospital bed and saw Piper and Poppy snuggled close together, as they'd been in her womb.

The nurse had advocated for "cobedding," suggesting that it might help the newborns sleep better and longer. Regan didn't know if the close proximity was responsible for their slumber now or if they were just exhausted from the whole birthing ordeal, but she was grateful that they were sleeping soundly.

And they weren't the only ones, she realized, when she saw a familiar figure slumped in a chair in the corner. "Connor?"

He was immediately awake, leaning forward to ask, "What do you need?"

She just shook her head. "What time is it?"

He glanced at his watch. "A few minutes after eleven."

Which meant that she'd been out for less than two hours. Still, she felt a little better now than when she'd closed her eyes. Not exactly rested and refreshed, but better.

Her husband hadn't left her side for a moment during her labor, which made her wonder, "Why are you still here?"

Thick, dark brows rose over warm brown eyes. "Where did you think I'd be?"

"Home," she suggested. "Where you could get some real sleep in a real bed."

He shrugged, his broad shoulders straining the seams of the Columbia Law sweatshirt—a Christmas gift from his brother—that he'd tugged over his head when she'd awakened him to say that her water had broken. "I didn't want to leave you."

Her throat tightened with emotion and she silently cursed the hormones that had kept her strapped into an emotional roller coaster for the past eight months. Since that long ago night when she'd first told Connor about her pregnancy, he'd been there for her, every step of the way. He'd held her hand at the first prenatal appointment— where they'd both been shocked to learn that she was going to have twins; he'd coached her through every contraction as she worked to bring their babies into the world; he'd even cut the umbilical cords—an act that somehow bonded them even more closely than the platinum bands they'd exchanged six months earlier.

"I think you couldn't stand to let the girls out of your sight," she teased now.

"That might be true, too." He covered her hand with his, squeezing gently. "Because they're every bit as beautiful as their mama."

She lifted her other hand to brush her hair away from her face. "I'd be afraid to even look in a mirror right now," she confided, all too aware that she hadn't washed her hair or even showered after sweating through the arduous labor.

"You're beautiful," Connor said again, and sounded as if he meant it.

She glanced away, uncertain how to respond. Over the past few months, there had been hints of something growing between them—aside from the girth of her belly—tempting Regan to hope that the marriage they'd entered into for the sake of their babies might someday become more.

Then a movement in the bassinet caught her eye. "It looks like Poppy's waking up."

He followed the direction of her gaze and smiled at the big yawn on the little girl's face. "Are you sure that's not Piper?"

"No," she admitted.

Although the twins weren't genetically identical, it wasn't easy to tell them apart. Poppy's hair was a shade darker than her sister's, and Piper had a half-moon-shaped birthmark beside her belly button, but of course, they were swaddled in blankets with caps on their heads, so neither telltale feature was visible right now.

He chuckled softly.

"Do you think she's hungry?" Regan asked worriedly.

The nurse had encouraged her to feed on demand, which meant putting the babies to her breast whenever they were awake and hungry. But her milk hadn't come in yet, so naturally Regan worried that her babies were always hungry because they weren't getting any sustenance.

"Let me change her diaper and then we'll see," Connor suggested.

She appreciated that he didn't balk at doing the messy jobs. Of course, parenthood was brand new to both of them, and changing diapers was still more of a novelty than a chore. With two infants, she suspected that would change quickly. The doting daddy might be ducking out of diaper changes before the week was out, but for now, she was grateful for the offer because it meant that her weary and aching body didn't have to get out of bed.

"She's so tiny," he said again, as he carefully lifted one of the pink-blanketed bundles out of the bassinet.

They were the first words he'd spoken when newborn Piper had been placed in his hands, his voice thick with a combination of reverence and fear.

"Not according to Dr. Amaro," she reminded him.

In fact, the doctor had remarked that the babies were good sizes for twins born two weeks early. Piper had weighed in at five pounds, eight ounces and measured eighteen and a half inches; Poppy had tipped the scale at five pounds, ten ounces and stretched out to an even eighteen inches. Still, she'd recommended that the new mom spend several days in the hospital with her babies to ensure they were feeding and growing before they went home.

But Regan agreed with Connor that the baby did look tiny, especially cradled as she was now in her daddy's big hands.

"And you were right," he said, as he unsnapped the baby's onesie to access her diaper. "This is Poppy."

Which only meant that the newborn didn't have a birthmark, not that her mother was particularly astute or intuitive.

Throughout her pregnancy, Regan had often felt out of her element and completely overwhelmed by the prospect of motherhood. When she was younger, several of her friends had earned money by babysitting, but Regan had never done so. She liked kids well enough; she just didn't have any experience with them.

She'd quickly taken to her niece—the daughter of her younger brother, Spencer. But Dani had been almost four years old the first time Regan met her, a little girl already walking and talking. A baby was a completely different puzzle—not just smaller but so much more fragile, unable to communicate except through cries that might mean she was hungry or wet or unhappy or any number of other things. And even after months spent preparing for the birth of her babies, Regan didn't feel prepared.

Thankfully, Connor didn't seem to suffer from the same worries and doubts. He warmed the wipe between his palms before folding back the wet diaper to gently clean the baby's skin.

"Did you borrow that plastic baby from our prenatal classes to practice on?" she wondered aloud.

He chuckled as he slid a clean diaper beneath Poppy's bottom. "No."

"Then how do you seem to know what you're doing already?"

"My brother's eight years younger than me," he reminded her. "And I changed enough of Deacon's diapers way back when to remember the basics of how it's done."

There was a photo in Brielle's baby album of Regan holding her infant sister in her lap and a bottle in the baby's mouth, but she didn't have any recollection of the event. She'd certainly never been responsible for taking care of her younger siblings. Instead, the routine child-care tasks had fallen to the family housekeeper, Celeste, because both Margaret and Ben Channing had spent most of their waking hours at Blake Mining.

But Connor's mom hadn't had the help of a live-in cook and housekeeper. If even half the stories that circulated around town were true, Faith Parrish worked three part-time jobs to pay the bills, often leaving her youngest son in the care of his big brother. Deacon's father had been in the picture for half a dozen years or so, but the general consensus in town was that he'd done nothing to help out at home and Faith was better off when he left. But everything Regan thought she knew about Connor's childhood was based on hearsay and innuendo, because even after six months of marriage, her husband remained tight-lipped about his family history.

Which didn't prevent her from asking: "Your father didn't help out much, did he?"

"Stepfather," he corrected automatically. "And no. He was always too busy."

"Doing what?" she asked, having heard that a serious fall had left the man with a back injury and unable to work.

"Watching TV and drinking beer," Connor said bluntly, as he slathered petroleum jelly on Poppy's bottom to protect her delicate skin before fastening the Velcro tabs on the new diaper.

"I guess you didn't miss him much when he left," she remarked.

He lifted the baby, cradling her gently against his chest as he carried her over to the bed. "I certainly didn't miss being knocked around."

She felt her skin go cold. "Your stepfather hit you?"

"Only when he was drinking."

Which he'd just admitted the man spent most of his time doing.

"How did I not know any of this?" she wondered aloud, as she unfastened her top to put the baby to her breast.

He shrugged again and turned away, as if to give her privacy.

If the topic of their conversation hadn't been so serious, Regan might have laughed at the idea of preserving even a shred of modesty with a man who'd watched the same baby now suckling at her breast come into the world between her widely spread legs.

"It's not something I like to talk about," he said, facing the closed blinds of the window.

"So why are you telling me now?" she asked curiously.

It was a good question, Connor acknowledged to himself.

He'd tried to bury that part of his past in the past. He didn't even like to think about those dark days when Dwayne Parrish had lived in the rented, ramshackle bungalow with him and his brother and their mother. To Dwayne, ruling with an iron fist wasn't just an expression but a point of pride most often made at his stepson's expense.

He turned back around, silently acknowledging that if he was going to have this conversation with his wife, they needed to have it face-to-face.

"Because part of me worries that, after living with him for seven years, I might have picked up his short fuse," he finally confided.

Regan immediately shook her head. "You didn't."

"We've only been married for six months. How can you know?"

"Because I know *you*," she said. "You are gentle and generous and giving."

"I hit him back once," he revealed.

She didn't seem bothered or even surprised by the admission. "Only once?"

"I never thought to fight back."

As a kid, he'd believed he was being disciplined for misbehavior. By the time he was old enough to question what was happening, he was so accustomed to being smacked around, it was no more or less than he expected.

"Not until he backhanded Deacon," he confided.

His little brother had been about seven years old when he'd accidentally kicked over a bottle of beer on the floor by Dwayne's recliner, spilling half its contents. Deacon's father had responded with a string of curses and a swift backhand that knocked the child off his feet.

"You wouldn't stand up for yourself, but you stood up for your brother," she mused.

"Someone had to," he pointed out. "He was just a kid."

"And how old were you?"

"Fifteen."

"Still a kid yourself," she remarked. "What did he… How did your stepfather respond?"

"He was furious with me—that I dared to interfere." And he'd expressed his anger with his fists and his feet, while Deacon cowered in the corner, sobbing. "But I guess one of our neighbors heard the ruckus and called the sheriff."

Faith had arrived home at almost the same time as the lawman. Connor didn't know if his mother would have found the strength to ask her husband to leave if Jed Traynor hadn't been there with his badge and gun. But he was and she did, and Dwayne opted to pack up and take off rather than spend the night—or maybe several years—in lockup.

"He left that night and never came back," Connor said.

"Is that when you decided that you wanted to wear a badge someday?" Regan asked.

"It was," he confirmed. "I know it sounds cheesy, but I wanted to help those who couldn't help themselves."

She shook her head. "I don't think it sounds cheesy. And that's how I know you're going to be an amazing dad."

"Because I finally stood up to my stepfather?"

"Because you didn't hesitate to do what was necessary to protect someone you care about," she clarified.

"There isn't anything I wouldn't do for my brother," Connor acknowledged.

And apparently, that included lying to his wife about the reasons he'd married her.

Chapter Two

As Regan climbed the steps toward the front door of the modest two-story on Larrea Drive that had been her home since she married the deputy, she knew that she should be accustomed to surprises by now. Over the past eight months, her life had been a seemingly endless parade of unexpected news and events.

It had all started with the plus sign in the little window on the home pregnancy test. The second—and even bigger surprise—had come in the form of not one but two heartbeats on the screen at her ultrasound appointment. The third—and perhaps the biggest shock of all—Connor Neal's unexpected marriage proposal, followed by her equally unexpected yes.

She hadn't known him very well when they exchanged vows, and if she hadn't been pregnant, she never would have said yes to his proposal. Of course, if she hadn't been pregnant, he never would have proposed. And though marriage had required a lot of adjustments from both of them, Connor had proven himself to be a devoted husband.

He'd been attentive to her wants and needs, considerate of her roller-coaster emotions and indulgent of her various pregnancy cravings. He'd attended childbirth classes, painted the babies' room, assembled their furniture and diligently researched car seat safety. And in the eight days that she'd spent in the hospital since their babies were born, he'd barely left her side.

But when she finally stepped inside the house, after fussing over the dog, whose whole back end was wagging with excitement as if she'd finally returned from eight weeks rather than only eight days away, she found another surprise.

The living room was filled with flowers and balloons and streamers. There was even a banner that read: *Welcome Home Mommy, Piper & Poppy!*

She looked at him, stunned. "When did you—"

"It wasn't my doing," he said, as he set the babies' car seats down inside the doorway.

Baxter immediately came to investigate, which meant sniffing the tiny humans all over, but he dutifully backed off when Connor held up a hand.

"Then who…" The rest of her question was forgotten as Regan looked past the bouquets of pink and white balloons to see a familiar figure standing there. "Ohmygod… *Brie.*"

Her sister smiled through watery eyes. "Surprise!"

Before Regan could say anything else, Brielle's arms were around her, hugging her tight. She held on, overwhelmed by so many emotions she didn't know whether to laugh or cry; she only knew that she was so glad and grateful her sister was home.

"Nobody told me you were coming," she said, when she'd managed to clear her throat enough to speak. She looked at Connor then. "Why didn't you tell me she was coming?" And back at Brielle again. "Why didn't *you* tell me you were coming?"

"When I spoke to you on the phone, I wasn't sure I'd be able to get any time off. But I needed to see you and your babies, so I decided that if I had to quit my job, I would."

Regan gasped, horrified, because she knew how much her sister loved working as a kindergarten teacher at a prestigious private school in Brooklyn. "Tell me you didn't quit your job."

Brie laughed. "No need to worry. I'm due back in the classroom Monday morning."

Which meant that they had less than four days together before her sister had to return to New York City. Four days was a short time, but it was more time than they'd had together in the seven years that had passed since Brielle moved away, and Regan would treasure every minute of it.

"Well, you're here now," she said.

"I'm here now," her sister agreed. "And I asked the rest of the family, who have already seen the babies, to give us some one-on-one time—with your husband and Piper and Poppy, of course." She moved closer to peek at the sleeping babies. "If they ever wake up."

"They'll be awake soon enough," Connor said. "And you'll have lots of time with them."

"Promise?" Brie asked.

He chuckled. "Considering that neither of them has slept for more than three consecutive hours since they were born, I feel confident making that promise. But for now, I'm going to take them upstairs so that you and your sister can relax and catch up."

Regan smiled her thanks as he exited the room with the babies, Baxter following closely on his heels, then she turned back to her sister. "When did you get in? Are you hungry? Thirsty?"

"I got in a few hours ago, I had a sandwich on the plane and, since you asked, I wouldn't mind a cup of tea to go with the cookies I picked up at The Daily Grind on the way from the airport, but I can make it."

"You stopped for cookies?"

"I made Spencer stop for cookies," Brie explained. "Because he picked me up from the airport. And because oatmeal chocolate chip are my favorite, too."

"Now I really want a cookie," Regan admitted. "But I no longer have the excuse of pregnancy cravings to indulge."

"Nursing moms need extra calories, too," her sister pointed out.

"In that case, what kind of tea do you want with your cookies?" she asked, already heading toward the kitchen.

Brie nudged her toward a chair at the table. "Your husband told you to relax."

"Making tea is hardly a strenuous task," Regan noted.

"Then it's one I should be able to handle." Her sister filled the electric kettle with water and plugged it in. "Where do you keep your mugs?"

"The cupboard beside the sink. Tea's on the shelf above the mugs."

Brie opened the cupboard and read the labels. "Spicy chai, pure peppermint, decaffeinated Earl Grey, honey lemon, country peach, blueberry burst, cranberry and orange, vanilla almond, apple and pear, and soothing chamomile." She glanced at her sister. "That's a lot of tea."

"I was a coffee addict," Regan confided. "The contents of that cupboard reflect my desperate effort to find something to take its place."

"Anything come close?" her sister wondered.

She shook her head. "But I'm thinking the vanilla almond would probably go well with the cookies."

"That works for me," Brie said, setting the box and two mugs on the counter.

Connor walked into the kitchen then, a baby monitor in hand. "Baxter missed his morning w-a-l-k so I'm going to take him out now, if you don't mind."

"Of course not," Regan assured him. "But why are you spelling?"

"Because you know how crazy he gets when I say the word."

Regan did know. In fact, Connor didn't even have to say the word; he only had to reach for the leash that hung on a hook by the door and Baxter went nuts—spinning in circles and yipping his excitement. But today the dog was nowhere to be found.

Brielle took a couple of steps back and peered up the staircase her brother-in-law had descended. "Is that first door the babies' room?"

"It's the master bedroom," Connor said, following her gaze. "But we've got the babies' bassinets set up in there for now."

"He's stretched out on the floor in front of the door," Brie said to Regan, so that her sister didn't have to get up to see what everyone else was seeing.

"And you were worried that he might be jealous of the babies," Regan remarked to her husband.

"He was abandoned when I found him," Connor explained. "So I had no idea if he'd ever been around kids or how he'd behaved with them if he had."

"What kind of dog is he?" Brie asked.

"A mutt," Connor said.

"A puggle," Regan clarified. "Though Connor refuses to acknowledge he has a designer dog."

"He has no papers, which makes him a mutt," her husband insisted.

"A puggle is part pug, part…beagle?" Brie guessed. Her sister nodded.

"That might explain why he's already so protective of the babies," Brie said. "Beagles are pack animals, and Piper and Poppy are now part of his pack."

"Say that five times fast," Regan teased. "And since when do you know so much about dogs?"

"I don't," her sister said. "But for a few months last year, I dated a vet who had a beagle. And a dachshund and a Great Dane."

"That's an eclectic assortment," Connor noted.

"He had three cats, too."

"Wait a minute," Regan said. "I'm still stuck on the fact that you dated this guy for a few months and I never heard anything about him until right now."

"Because there was nothing to tell," her sister said.

"Baxter," Connor called, obviously preferring to walk rather than hear about his sister-in-law's dating exploits.

The dog obediently trotted down the stairs, though he hesitated at the bottom. His tail wagged when Connor held up the leash, but he turned his head to glance back at where the babies were sleeping.

"Piper and Poppy will be fine," Connor promised. "Their mommy and Auntie Brie will be here if they need anything while we're out."

Of course, the dog probably didn't understand what his master was saying, but he seemed reassured enough to let Connor hook the leash onto his collar.

"I won't be too long," Connor said, then reached across the counter to flip the switch on the kettle.

Brie looked at her sister. "How long were you going to let me wait for the water to boil before telling me that there was a switch?"

"Only a little while longer."

Connor chuckled as he led Baxter to the door.

"So tell me when and how you met the hunky deputy," Brie said, as she poured the finally boiling water into the mugs.

"I've known Connor since high school. He was a year ahead of me, but we were in the same math class because I accelerated through some of my courses."

"I remember now," Brie said. "He was a scrawny guy with a surly attitude who you tutored in calculus."

She was grateful her sister didn't refer to him as the bastard kid of "Faithless Faith"—a cruel nickname that had followed Connor's mother to her grave. Regan had never met Faith Neal—later Faith Parrish—but she knew of her reputation.

In her later years, Faith had been a hardworking single mom devoted to her two sons, but people still remembered her as a wild teenager who'd snuck out after curfew, hung with a bad crowd and smoked cigarettes and more.

Some people believed she was desperately looking for the love she'd never known at home. Others were less charitable in their assessment and made her the punchline to a joke. If a man suffered any kind of setback, such as the loss of a job or the breakup of a relationship, others would encourage him to "Have Faith." That advice was usually followed by raucous laughter and the rejoinder: "Everyone else in town has had her."

"He sure did fill out nicely," Brie remarked now. "Was it those broad shoulders that caught your eye? Or the sexy dent in his square chin? Because I'm guessing it wasn't his kitchen decor."

Regan reached into the bakery box for a cookie. "This room is an eyesore, isn't it?"

"Or are white melamine cupboards with red plastic handles retro-chic?"

"Connor's saving up to renovate."

"Saving up?" Brie echoed, sounding amused. "I guess that means he didn't marry you for your money."

"He married me because I was pregnant," Regan told her. Because when a bride gave birth six months after the ring was put on her finger, what was the point in pretending otherwise?

"Well, if you had to get knocked up, at least it was by a guy who was willing to do the right thing."

"Hmm," Regan murmured in apparent agreement.

Brie broke off a piece of cookie. "I would have come home for your wedding, if you'd asked."

"We eloped in Reno," Regan told her.

"Doesn't that count as a wedding?"

She shook her head. "Weddings take time to plan, and I didn't want to be waddling down the aisle."

"I'm sure you didn't waddle," her sister said loyally.

"I showed you my belly when we Facetimed, so you know I was huge. I was waddling before the end of my fifth month."

"Well, you were carrying two babies," Brie acknowledged. She chewed on another bite of cookie before she asked, "What did the folks think about your elopement?"

"They were surprisingly supportive. Or maybe just grateful that their second and third grandchildren wouldn't be born out of wedlock."

Their first was Spencer's daughter, but he hadn't even known about Dani's existence until her mother was killed in an accident. He'd given up his career on the rodeo circuit to assume custody, then moved back to Haven with his little girl and fallen in love with Kenzie Atkins, who had been Brielle's BFF in high school.

"They were a lot less happy to learn that I was pregnant," Regan confided to her sister now. " Dad's exact words were, 'And you were supposed to be the smart one.'"

Brie winced. "That's harsh. Although it's true that you're the smart one."

"They don't let dummies into Columbia," Regan pointed out.

"True," her sister said again. "But no one I met at Columbia is as smart as you." She selected another cookie from the box. "What did Mom say?"

"You know Mom," Regan said. "Always practical and looking for the solution to a problem."

Brie's expression darkened. "Because a baby is a problem to be solved and not a miracle to be celebrated."

"I like to think they were happy about the babies but concerned about my status in town as an unwed mother," Regan said, though even she wasn't convinced it was true. "You know how people here like to gossip."

"And then Connor stepped up to ensure the legitimacy of his babies and all was right in the world?" Brie asked, her tone dubious.

"Well, Dad was happy that Connor had done the right thing—at least, from his perspective. Mom made no secret of the fact that she thinks Connor and I aren't well-suited."

"How about *you*?" Brie asked. "Are you happy with the way everything turned out?"

"I never thought I could be this happy," Regan responded sincerely. Not that her marriage was perfect, but she was confident that she'd made the right choice for her babies—and hopeful that it would prove to be the right choice for her and her husband, too.

"I'm glad."

It was the tone rather than the words that tripped Regan's radar. "So why don't you sound glad?" she asked her sister.

Brie shrugged. "I guess I'm just thinking about the fact that everyone around me seems to be having babies," she explained. "Two of my colleagues are off on mat leave right now, a third is due at the end of the summer and another just announced that she's expecting."

"That's a lot of babies. But still, you're a little young for your biological clock to be ticking already," Regan noted.

"I'm not in any rush," Brie said. "But I do hope that someday I'll have everything you've got—a husband who loves me and the babies we've made together. Although I'd be happier if they came one at a time."

Regan managed a smile, despite the tug of longing in her own heart—and the twinge of guilt that she wasn't being completely honest with her sister. "I have no doubt that your time will come."

"Maybe. But until then, I'll be happy to dote on your beautiful babies."

"You'd be able to dote a lot more if you didn't live twenty-five hundred miles away," she felt compelled to point out.

"I know," her sister acknowledged. "I love New York, my job, my coworkers and all the kids. And I have a great apartment that I share with wonderful friends. But there are times when I miss being here. When I miss you and Kenzie and—well, I miss you and Kenzie."

Regan's smile came more easily this time. "So come home," she urged.

Brie shook her head. "There's one elementary school in Haven and it already has a kindergarten teacher."

"That's what's holding you back?" Regan asked skeptically. "A lack of job opportunities?"

"It's a valid consideration," her sister said. Then, when she heard a sound emanate from the monitor, "Is that one of my nieces that I hear now?"

Regan chuckled, even as her breasts instinctively responded to the sound of the infant stirring. "You know, most people don't celebrate the sound of a baby crying," she remarked.

"But doting aunts are always happy to help with snuggles and cuddles."

"And diaper changes?"

"Whatever you need," Brie promised.

Chapter Three

As soon as Connor and Baxter stepped outside, the dog put his nose to the ground and set off, eager to explore all the sights and smells. They had a specific route that they walked in the mornings and a different, longer route they usually followed later in the day. At the end of the street, Baxter instinctively turned east, to follow the longer route.

"We're doing the short route this afternoon," he said. Although he enjoyed their twice-daily walks almost as much as the dog, he didn't want to leave Regan for too long on her first day back from the hospital.

He knew it was silly, especially considering that her sister was there to help with anything she might need help with. But Connor was the one who'd been with her through every minute of twenty-two hours of labor and for most of the eight days since, and he was feeling protective of the new mom and babies—and maybe a little proprietary.

Baxter gave him a look that, on a human, might have been disapproving, but the dog obediently turned in the opposite direction.

Connor started to jog, hoping to compensate for the abbreviated course with more intense exercise. Baxter trotted beside him, tongue hanging out of his mouth, tail wagging.

He lifted a hand in response to Cal Thompson's wave

and nodded to Sherry Witmer, who was carrying an armload of groceries into her house. It had taken some time, but he was finally beginning to feel as if he was part of the community he'd moved into three years earlier.

There were still some residents who pretended they didn't see him when he walked by. People like Joyce Cline, the retired music teacher whose disapproval of "that no-good Neal boy" went back to his days in high school. And Rick Beamer, whose daughter Connor had gone out with exactly twice, more than a dozen years earlier.

But he was pleased to note that the Joyce Clines and Rick Beamers were outnumbered in the neighborhood. The day that Connor moved in, he'd barely started to unpack when Darlene and Ron Grassley were at his door to introduce themselves—and to give him a tray of stuffed peppers. An hour later, Lois Barkowsky had stopped by with a plate of homemade brownies—assuring him that they weren't the "funny kind," even though recreational marijuana use was now legal in Nevada. He told her that he was aware of the law and thanked her for the goodies.

Over the next few weeks, he'd gotten to know most of the residents of Larrea Street. When he'd taken in Baxter and started walking on a regular basis, he'd met several more who lived in the surrounding area.

Estela Lopez was one of those people, and as he and Baxter turned onto Chaparral Street, they saw the older woman coming toward them. At seventy-nine years of age, she kept herself active, walking every morning before breakfast and every evening after supper—and apparently also at other times in between.

"Oh, this is a treat," she said, clearly delighted to see them.

In response to the word *treat*, Baxter immediately

assumed the "sit" position and waited expectantly. She chuckled and reached into the pocket of her coat for one of the many biscuits she always had on hand. Baxter gobbled up the offering.

An avid dog lover who'd had to say goodbye to her seventeen-year-old Jack Russell the previous winter, Estela worried that she wasn't able-bodied enough to take on the responsibility of another animal. Instead, she gave her love and doggy biscuits to the neighborhood canines who wandered by.

"How are you doing, Mrs. Lopez?" Connor asked her.

"I'm eager to see pictures of your girls," the old woman told him.

Connor dutifully pulled out his phone. "They came home today."

"Eight days later." She shook her head. "I remember when they kicked you out of the hospital after only a day or two. Of course, most people couldn't afford to stay any longer than that."

Which they both knew wasn't a concern for his wife, whose family had not only paid the hospital bill but made a significant donation to the maternity ward as a thank you to the staff for their care of Regan and the twins.

He opened the screen and scrolled through numerous images of Piper and Poppy—a few individual snaps of each girl, others of them together and a couple with their mom.

"Oh, my, they are so precious," Estela proclaimed. "And Regan doesn't look like she labored for twenty-something hours."

"Twenty-two," Connor said. "And she did. And she was a trouper."

"You're a lucky man, Deputy Neal."

"I know it," he assured her.

Baxter nudged her leg with his nose, as if to remind her of his presence. She obligingly reached down and scratched behind his ears.

"I heard your sister-in-law made a surprise visit from New York City."

"Well, there's obviously nothing wrong with your hearing," Connor teased.

"I was at The Daily Grind, having coffee with Dolores Lorenzo, when she stopped in to pick up a dozen oatmeal chocolate chip cookies," Estela confided.

"Regan's favorite."

"I almost didn't recognize her—Brielle, I mean," Estela clarified. "Of course, she's only been back a few times since she moved out East—it's gotta be about seven years ago, I'd guess. And even when she came back for Spencer and Kenzie's wedding, she only stayed a couple of days."

"She's only here for a few days now, too," Connor noted.

"Is she staying with you or at that fancy house up on the hill?"

That fancy house up on the hill was the description frequently ascribed to the three-story stone-and-brick mansion owned by his in-laws. The street was called Miners' Pass, and it was the most exclusive—and priciest—address in town.

"With us," he said. "She wants to spend as much time as possible with Regan and the twins."

"Of course she does," Estela agreed. "I can't wait to take a peek at the little darlings myself, but I'll give your wife some time to settle in first. Although my kids are all grown-up now—and most of my grandkids, too—I remember how stressful it was in those early days, trying to respond to all the new demands of motherhood—and I only had to deal with one baby at a time."

"Regan would love to see you," Connor said. "Especially after she's had a chance to catch up on her rest."

"Well, I'm not waiting until the twins' second birthday," she told him, sneaking another biscuit out of her pocket for Baxter.

"Please don't tell me it's going to be that long before Piper and Poppy sleep through the night."

"Probably not," she acknowledged. "But dealing with the needs of infants requires a special kind of endurance—which I don't have anymore, so I'm going to get these weary bones of mine inside where it's warm."

"You do that," he said.

She started up the drive toward her house, then paused to turn back. "But don't let those babies exhaust all your energy—" she cautioned, with a playful wink "—because new moms have needs that require attention, too."

"I'll keep that in mind," Connor promised, then he waited to ensure his old neighbor was safely inside before heading on his way again.

But the truth was, if his wife had any such needs, Connor would likely be the last to know. Although he and Regan presented themselves as happy newlyweds whenever they were in public together, they mostly lived separate lives behind closed doors. Sure, it was an unorthodox arrangement for expectant parents, but it had worked for them.

Until his brother came home for the Christmas holidays.

Because, of course, Deacon expected to sleep in his own room. He had no reason to suspect that his brother's marriage wasn't a love match—although he was undoubtedly smart enough to realize that his sister-in-law's rapidly expanding belly was the reason they'd married in such a hurry—and Connor didn't ever want him to know the truth.

So for the sixteen days—and fifteen nights—that his brother was home, Connor moved his belongings back into the master bedroom to maintain the charade that his and Regan's marriage was a normal one.

The days hadn't really been a problem—especially as Regan continued to work her usual long hours in the finance department at Blake Mining. But the nights, when Connor was forced to share a bed with his wife, were torture.

He made a valiant effort to stay on his side of the mattress, to ignore the fragrant scent of her hair spread out over the pillow next to his own, and the soft, even sound of breath moving in and out of her lungs, causing her breasts to rise and fall in a steady rhythm. But it was impossible to pretend she wasn't there, especially when she tossed and turned so frequently.

She apologized to him for her restlessness, acknowledging that it was becoming more and more difficult to find a comfortable position as her belly grew rounder. Connor knew she was self-conscious about her "babies bump," but he honestly thought she looked amazing. He knew it was a common belief that all pregnant women were beautiful, though he'd never paid much attention to expectant mothers before he married Regan. But he couldn't deny that his pregnant wife was stunning.

Of course, he'd always believed she was beautiful—and maybe a little intimidating in her perfection. In addition to the inches on her waistline, pregnancy had added a natural glow to her cheeks and warmth to her smile, making her look softer and more approachable. And as the weeks turned into months, Connor realized that he was in danger of falling for the woman he'd married.

During one of those endlessly long nights that his brother was home, Connor pretended to be asleep so that Regan would relax and sleep, too. But he froze when he heard her breath catch, then slowly release.

"Are you okay?" he asked, breaking the silence as he rolled over to face her.

"I'm fine," she said. Then she took his hand and pressed it against the curve of her belly.

He was so startled by the impulsive gesture, he nearly pulled his hand away. But then he felt it—a subtle nudge against his palm. Then another nudge.

His other hand automatically came up so that he had both on her belly as his heart filled with joy and wonder. "Is that...your babies?"

"Our babies," she correctly quickly. "Or at least one of them." Then she moved his second hand. "That's the other one."

"Oh, wow." He couldn't help but smile at this proof that there were tiny human beings growing inside her. Sure, he'd seen them on the ultrasound, but feeling tangible evidence of their movements was totally different than watching them on a screen. "Apparently, they've decided that Mommy's bedtime is their playtime," he noted.

"According to the baby books, it's not uncommon for an expectant mother to be more aware of her baby's movements at night," she told him.

"Or for babies to be more active at night, as their mother's movements during the day rock them to sleep," he remarked.

"You've been reading the books, too," she realized.

"I can't wait to meet your—our—" he corrected himself this time "—little ones."

"I'm not sure how little they are anymore," Regan said. "I know that I'm certainly not."

"You're beautiful," he said sincerely.

"You don't have to placate me. I know I look like I swallowed a beach ball."

"You look like you're pregnant—and you're beautiful."

She looked at him then, and their gazes held for a long, lingering moment in the darkness of the night.

Afterward, he couldn't have said who made the first move. He only knew that she was suddenly in his arms, and her lips were locked with his in a kiss that was so much hotter than he'd imagined.

Because yes, there had been occasions since they'd exchanged vows that he'd found himself wondering what it might be like if their marriage was more than a piece of paper. There had been times when their eyes had locked, and he'd thought that maybe she wouldn't mind if he breached the distance between them to kiss her, that maybe she even wished he would.

But he'd always held back, because he knew that if he was wrong and the attraction he felt was not reciprocated, their living arrangement would become so much more awkward.

Neither of them was holding back now.

She wriggled closer—as close as her belly would allow. He cupped her breasts through the soft cotton nightshirt. His thumbs brushed over the peaks of her already taut nipples, and she gasped. "Oh, yes." She whispered the words of encouragement against his lips. "Touch me, please."

He couldn't respond, because she was kissing him again.

And he was touching her, tracing the luscious contours of her body, learning what she liked and what she really liked by the way she arched and sighed.

Their lips clung as their hands eagerly searched and explored. The encounter was as hot and passionate as it was surprising—and it might have led to more if he hadn't suddenly remembered that theirs wasn't a real marriage and recalled that all the baby books he'd been reading talked about how the hormonal changes a woman went through during pregnancy could increase or decrease her sexual appetites. Add to that the forced proximity of their sleeping arrangements and the excitement of the holidays, and he had to wonder how much those factors were influencing her reactions right now.

But did it matter what was motivating her sudden desire?

Or did it only matter that she wanted him—as he wanted her?

Unfortunately, his body and his brain were in disagreement on the answers to those questions.

And his conscience—reminding him of the deal he'd made with her father—won out.

Because even if making love was her *choice, it couldn't be an informed choice so long as there were secrets between them. And there was a very big secret between them.*

For the remainder of the holidays, he'd stayed up late every night to ensure Regan was asleep before he slid between the sheets of their shared bed. Thankfully, Deacon returned to Columbia early in the New Year, allowing his brother and sister-in-law to once again retreat to their respective corners. But there was no "back to normal" for Connor, because there was no way he could forget the passionate kiss they'd shared. Or stop wondering what their marriage might be like now if he hadn't put on the brakes that night.

And with her sister visiting, he would be forced to share his wife's bed again.

Of course, there was no question of anything happening between them only eight days after she'd given birth. But he suspected that knowledge wouldn't prevent his body from responding to her nearness, and he prepared himself for the sleepless nights ahead that had nothing to do with the demands of their newborn babies.

Regan and Brielle were on the sofa in the living room, each with a baby in her arms, when Connor and Baxter returned from their walk.

"You weren't gone very long," Regan remarked.

"We did the short route," Connor said, unhooking the dog's leash to hang it up again.

Baxter immediately ran to his bowl for a drink of water.

"Did you see Mrs. Lopez?" she asked.

He nodded. "And Baxter got two treats."

"Spoiled dog," she said affectionately. "What about you?" she asked her husband. "Did you get any treats?"

He shook his head.

"Well, then it's lucky you did the short route," she told him. "Because there are still a couple of cookies left in the bakery box on the counter."

"Only a couple out of the dozen that Brie picked up at The Daily Grind?" he teased.

"How did you know where I got the cookies? And how many?" Brie wondered.

"Mrs. Lopez was in the café when you stopped by," he admitted.

"You've been away so long you've forgotten the many joys of small-town living," Regan remarked sardonically.

"Because having everyone know your business is a joy?" her sister asked skeptically.

"Having a freezer full of casseroles courtesy of neighbors who want you to be able to focus on your babies is a joy."

"I'll reserve judgment on that—until after dinner," Brie said. "Just don't expect me to eat anything called tuna surprise, because I'm not a fan of tuna and I don't think anyone should ingest something with *surprise* in the name."

"No tuna surprise tonight," Connor promised. "Celeste dropped off a tray of lasagna, a loaf of garlic bread and a bowl of green salad."

Brie gave her sister a sidelong glance. "Now who's spoiled?"

Regan just grinned.

Over dinner Brielle entertained them with stories about her job and her life in New York. Though Regan was in regular contact with her sister via telephone and email, she'd missed this in-person connection. Connor seemed content to listen to their spirited conversation while he rubbed Baxter's belly with his foot beneath the table.

It seemed a strange coincidence to Regan that her sister and his brother were both currently living in the Big Apple. If their circumstances had been different—and they didn't have two newborn babies—she might have suggested that they take a trip to New York to visit their respective siblings. But their circumstances weren't different, and she didn't envision any joint travel plans anywhere in their immediate future.

"There's an Italian restaurant near our place—Nonna's Kitchen—that my roommate Grace would swear has the best lasagna she's ever tasted." Brie dug her fork into her pasta again. "I told her that she only thought it was the best because she's never had Celeste's lasagna, but even I'd forgotten how good this really is."

"Her chicken cacciatore is even better," Connor noted.

"Apples and oranges," Brie said. "Though I would say they're both equally delicious."

By the time they'd finished eating, Piper was awake and wanting her dinner, so Regan and Brie went to deal with the babies while Connor washed the dishes and tidied the kitchen. He walked into the living room as Regan lifted a hand to her mouth, attempting to stifle a yawn.

"I'm sorry," she said to her sister.

"I should be the one to apologize," Brielle said. "You just got home from the hospital after giving birth barely more than a week ago—it's a wonder you're still awake."

"And since the babies are sleeping…" Connor began.

"I should be, too," his wife said, finishing the recitation of the advice all the doctors and nurses had given to her. "And I will, as soon as I make up the bed in the spare room—"

"Already done," he said.

"You didn't have to go to any trouble," Brielle protested. "I would have been happy camping on the sofa with a blanket and pillow."

"It wasn't any trouble at all," Connor assured her.

She hugged him then. "You are, without a doubt, my absolute favorite brother-in-law."

"I'm your only brother-in-law," he remarked dryly.

Brielle grinned. "And that's why you're my favorite."

Regan couldn't help but smile, too, as she listened to the banter between them. She was pleased that Brie had so readily accepted Connor as part of the family, especially because she knew he hadn't been welcomed with open arms by her mom and dad.

But she wasn't worried about his relationship with her parents right now—a bigger and more immediate concern was the fact that she had to share a bed with her husband tonight.

Chapter Four

"Does your sister have everything she needs?" Connor asked, when Regan entered the master bedroom a few minutes later.

"I think so." She paused at the bassinet to check on the babies. "I still can't believe that she's here."

"You're surprised that your sister wanted to see you and meet her nieces?"

"No," she admitted. "But I am surprised that the wanting was stronger than her determination to stay away."

"I'm obviously missing something," he realized.

She nodded. "Brie moved to New York seven years ago and she's only been home twice since. The first was for my grandmother's funeral, the second—four years later—for Spencer and Kenzie's wedding."

"What's the story?" he wondered.

"I'm not sure I know all of it," his wife said. "But even if I did, it's not my story to tell."

"Well, whatever her reasons for staying away for so long, she's here now."

"And I'm grateful," Regan told him. "But I wouldn't have minded if she'd chosen to stay at our parents' place, where she would have had her pick of half a dozen empty guest rooms."

"Here she can maximize her time with you and Piper and Poppy."

"I know," she agreed, lowering her voice. "I just feel

bad, because I could hardly tell her that she's kicking you out of your room."

Actually, it was his brother's room, but Connor had been sleeping in it since his wife had moved in at the beginning of October—save for the two endlessly long weeks that Deacon was home over the Christmas holidays.

"It's only for a few nights," he said philosophically.

"You're right," she agreed, pulling open a dresser drawer to retrieve a nightgown.

But Regan knew that her brother-in-law would be home again at the beginning of May—and not just for a couple of weeks but the whole summer this time. And she had to wonder how long she and Connor would be able to maintain a physical distance while they were sharing a bed—or even if they'd want to.

Because even now, when her body was still aching and exhausted from the experience of childbirth, it was also hyper-aware of his nearness, stirring with desire.

In defense against this unexpected yearning, she went into the bathroom to change and brush her teeth, and when she came back, she saw that Connor had pulled on an old T-shirt and a pair of sleep pants. The clothes covered most of her husband's body but couldn't disguise his size or strength.

She estimated his height at six feet four inches, because even when she added heels to her five-foot-eight-inch frame, he stood several inches above her. His shoulders were broad, his pecs sculpted, his arms strong. He had a long-legged stride and moved with purpose—a man who knew where he was going and inevitably drew glances of female admiration along the way.

He had an attractive face on top of those broad shoulders. Lean and angular with a square jaw, straight brows and a slightly crooked nose. His lips, though exquisitely shaped, were usually compressed in a thin line. Many people attributed his serious demeanor to his serious job in law enforcement, but Regan had known him since high school, so she knew that his somber outlook predated his employment. The little he'd told her about his youth confirmed that he hadn't had much to smile about while he was growing up. Yet despite his often stern and imposing expression, his eyes—the color of dark, melted chocolate—were invariably kind.

Her husband was a good man. She had no doubts about that. It was their future together that was a whole series of questions without answers—none of which she was going to get tonight so she might as well climb into bed and get some sleep.

But first, she checked on the babies one more time. They were sleeping peacefully for the moment, each with one arm stretched out toward the other, so that their fingertips were touching.

"I want to believe that they'll be the best of friends someday, but I think they already are," she said quietly.

"Like you and your sister?"

"We weren't always so close," she admitted. "Of course, there are four years between us, and only fourteen minutes between Piper and Poppy."

He moved so that he was standing directly behind Regan to peer down at the sleeping babies. "Not to mention that they were roommates in your womb for thirty-six weeks."

"We probably didn't need two bassinets," she acknowledged. "By the time they're too big to share this one, they'll be ready for a crib."

"So we'll put the other one downstairs," he suggested.

"That's a good idea."

"I have one every once in a while."

She tipped her head back against his shoulder and looked up at him. "Was getting married a good idea?"

"One of my best," he assured her.

"We'll see if you still think so when they wake you up several times in the night."

"In order to be woken up, we first have to go to sleep."

She nodded and, with a last glance at her babies, tiptoed to "her" side of the bed. The queen-size mattress had been plenty big enough when she was the only one sleeping in it, but it seemed to have shrunk to less than half its usual size now that Connor would be sharing it.

For the past six and a half months, he'd been a strong and steady presence by her side—if not in her bed. And she was sincerely grateful for everything he'd done and continued to do.

She'd always prided herself on being a strong, independent woman. She'd never balked at a challenge or let any obstacles deter her; she didn't need anyone to hold her hand or bolster her courage. Not until that plus sign appeared in the little window of her home pregnancy test.

Somehow, that tiny symbol changed everything. She suddenly felt scared and vulnerable and alone, unprepared and ill-equipped for the future.

Then Connor had shown up at her ultrasound appointment and changed everything again—but in a good way this time.

She remembered taking a quick look around the waiting room of the maternal health clinic and noting that many of the seats were already taken by couples sitting with their heads close. No doubt they were whispering their thoughts about the journey into parenthood they were taking together. And that was great for them, she'd acknowledged. But she didn't need a husband or boyfriend or partner. She could do this on her own.

So she'd stepped up to the counter and given her name to the receptionist, then taken a seat as directed—a single woman in the midst of countless happy couples.

But that was okay because she was excited enough for two people, because this was her first ultrasound. A first look at her baby. There were still some days that she wondered if her pregnancy was real or just a dream. As shocked and scared as she'd felt when she'd seen the result of the home pregnancy test, her brain didn't seem able to connect that little plus sign with the concept of a baby.

Even after Dr. Amaro had confirmed the results of that test, Regan still had trouble accepting that a tiny life was taking shape in her womb. The queasiness and sore breasts that came a few days later were more tangible evidence, but still not irrefutable proof.

Or maybe she'd just been lingering in denial because the prospects of childbirth and parenthood—especially as a single mom—were so damn scary.

She hadn't had the first clue about being a mother. Numbers and balance sheets and cost flow statements were second nature, but babies were a completely foreign entity. Her sister had always wanted to get married and have a houseful of kids. Regan's lifelong dream had been to work at Blake Mining. She didn't *not* want kids, she just hadn't given the idea much thought. And, whenever she *had* thought about it, she'd always assumed it would happen after she'd fallen in love and married the father of her future children.

But there was a saying about life happening while you were making other plans, and the tiny life growing inside of her was proof of that.

So while being a single mom was never part of her

plan, she'd vowed to give it her best effort. And she would do it alone, because she had no other choice.

As a defense against the threat of tears, she'd grabbed a magazine from the table beside her. She opened the cover and began to flip through the pages, not paying any attention to the photos or articles, unable to focus on any of the words on the page where she paused.

"'Preparing Your Child for Kindergarten','" a familiar voice read from over her shoulder. "I know there's an old adage about planning ahead, but don't you think you should focus on getting ready for the birth before you worry about your baby's first day of school?"

She closed the cover of the magazine as Connor lowered himself into the vacant seat beside her. "What are you doing here?"

"I didn't want you to be alone for this."

"But how did you even know I'd be here?"

"You mentioned the appointment when our paths crossed at The Trading Post."

"And you remembered?" she asked incredulously.

"Well, you looked like you were ready to have a meltdown in the frozen food aisle, and I realized you were overwhelmed by the idea of doing this alone, so I noted the date in my calendar app."

That he'd done so and made the trip to Battle Mountain to be with her was a surprise—and her eyes filled with tears of relief and gratitude.

Because right now, at least in this moment, she wasn't alone.

"I should probably tell you to go, that I don't need someone to hold my hand," she said. "But...I'm so glad to see you."

He reached for her hand and linked their fingers together. "Everything's going to be okay."

It was a ridiculous thing to say—the words a promise she knew he shouldn't make and couldn't keep. And yet, she already felt so much better just because he was there. Connor Neal—former bad boy turned sheriff's deputy— so strong and steady, an unexpected rock to cling to in the storm of emotion that threatened to consume her.

"Regan Channing."

She rose to her feet, her heart knocking against her ribs.

Connor stood with her and gave her hand a reassuring squeeze.

"Are you going to come in?" she asked.

"Do you want *me to come in?"*

She nodded, surprised to realize that she did.

The technician had introduced herself as Lissa and led them to an exam room.

She'd explained that they were there to take a first look at the baby, reassuring Regan that Dr. Amaro didn't have any specific concerns, so the primary purpose of the scan was to take some measurements to get an accurate estimate of her due date.

When Regan had stretched out on the table and lifted her shirt, Lissa squirted gel onto her belly and spread it around with a wand-like device she'd called a transducer, explaining that the sound waves would be converted into black and white images on the screen and provide an image of the baby.

Regan had reached for Connor's hand again, and squeezed it a little tighter, as both anticipation and apprehension swelled inside her.

"Now I really have to pee," she said, as Lissa pressed the transducer against her belly and began to move it around.

"Sorry," the technician said. "The full bladder can be

uncomfortable for the expectant mom, but it does allow us to get a better picture of the uterus and baby."

She continued to move the device—and press on Regan's bladder—as she made notes of measurements.

"The baby's heartbeat is strong and steady," Lissa said.

Regan tried to focus on the screen, but it was hard to see through the tears that blurred her eyes. Again. Since she'd taken that pregnancy test, she'd been quick to tears no matter what she was feeling. Happy. Scared. Angry. Sad.

"Actually...both heartbeats are strong and steady," Lissa remarked.

Regan blinked. "I'm sorry... What?"

The technician smiled. "Yeah, that's the usual reaction I get when I tell an expectant mother she's going to have twins."

"Twins?" Regan echoed, uncomprehending.

Lissa moved the wand over her patient's abdomen with one hand and pointed at the monitor with the other. "There's one...and there's the other one."

"Ohmygod." Regan looked at Connor—as if he might somehow be able to make sense at what she was seeing, because her brain refused to do so. "There are two babies in there."

"I can see that," he acknowledged, sounding as stunned as she felt.

"I can't have two babies," she protested. "I don't know what to do with one."

"You'll figure it out," he assured her.

As Regan's eyes drifted shut now, she finally believed that she would figure it out—so long as Connor was by her side.

* * *

Lying next to his wife in bed, Connor found himself also recalling the fateful day that he'd made the trip to Battle Mountain for Regan's ultrasound appointment.

She'd asked him why he'd shown up at the clinic, and the answer might have been as simple as that he knew she was feeling a little scared and overwhelmed and he wanted to be there for her—as she'd been there for him when he'd been struggling in twelfth grade calculus. Or maybe he hadn't completely gotten over the crush he'd had on her when she tutored him in high school. Regardless of his reasons, seeing how freaked out she was at the sight of those two tiny little blobs on the screen—twins!—he'd been doubly (Ha! Ha!) glad that he'd cleared his schedule for the morning.

"You still look a little shell-shocked," he'd noted, as they walked out of the clinic.

"Only a little?"

He'd smiled at that. "Let's take a walk. There's an ice cream shop just down the street."

"I don't think a scoop of chocolate chip cookie dough is the answer."

"Considering the circumstances, I was going to suggest two scoops," he told her.

Her eyes had filled with tears then. "That's not funny."

"You're right. I'm sorry." He'd pulled a tissue out of his pocket and offered it to her. "But I have to admit—it was pretty cool to see those two little hearts beating on the screen."

"Sure," she'd agreed. "If cool is another word for terrifying."

"What are you afraid of?"

"Everything."

"C'mon." He slid his arm across her shoulders and steered her down the street.

She hadn't protested. She hadn't even asked where they were going—a sure sign to Connor that she was preoccupied with her own thoughts. At least until he'd stopped in front of Scoops Ice Cream Shoppe.

"You don't have to do this," she said, when he'd opened the door for her to enter. "I'm not one of those women who tries to drown my worries with copious amounts of chocolate."

"Well, I *am* one of those guys who believes that ice cream is essential for any celebration."

"What are we celebrating?"

"I would have thought that was obvious," he'd said. "But since you're feeling a little overwhelmed by the prospect of impending motherhood right now, we can focus on something else."

"Such as?"

He'd gestured to the sky outside. "The sun is shining."

"Do you celebrate every sunny day with ice cream?"

"I might, if we had a Scoops in Haven," he told her.

Regan had managed a smile as she moved closer to view the offerings in the glass freezer case.

She'd opted for a single scoop of chocolate chip cookie dough in a cup. He'd topped a scoop of rocky road with another of chocolate in a waffle cone. And they'd sat across from each other on red vinyl padded benches with a Formica table between them.

He'd enjoyed his ice cream in silence for several minutes, giving her some time to sort out whatever thoughts were creating the furrow between her brows.

"You're not eating your ice cream," he'd commented, as she continued to mush the frozen concoction with her spoon.

She lifted the utensil to her lips. "I was just starting to get my head around the fact that I was going to have a baby, only to find out that I'm going to have *two*," she'd finally shared.

"All the more reason to tell your family sooner rather than later," he'd pointed out. Because he knew that he was the only person she'd confided in about her pregnancy so far.

She'd nodded and swallowed another mouthful of ice cream. "I know you're right. I just can't imagine how they're going to react." Then she shook her head. "No, that's not true. I'm pretty sure my dad's going to flip."

Her comment had prompted him to ask, "Does your father have a temper?"

"Not that most people would know," she'd said. "Because it takes a lot to make him lose his cool, but I suspect my big news will do the trick."

He'd frowned at that. Even in a relatively quiet town like Haven, he'd responded to his share of domestic violence calls—and he knew, better than anyone, that some of the worst abusers presented a completely benevolent persona to the outside world.

"Would he… Has he ever…hit you?" he'd asked cautiously.

Regan's eyes had gone round with shock. "Ohmygod—no! He would never… I didn't mean… No," she'd said again.

Her automatic and emphatic denial rang true, which had been an enormous relief to Connor.

"When I said that he had a temper, I only meant that he'll probably yell a little," she'd confided. "Or a lot. But far worse than the yelling is that he'll be disappointed in me."

"And your mom?" he'd wondered aloud.

"She tends to be a little more practical—the 'no sense crying over spilled milk' type," Regan had told him. "She'll want to start interviewing nannies right away, so that I can get back to work as soon as possible, because nothing is as important to her as Blake Mining. And then we'll probably argue about that, because I may not know a lot about parenting, but I know I don't want a stranger raising my babies. I mean, I don't plan to be a stay-at-home mom forever, but I don't want my children to have to visit my office if they want to see me."

Which he'd guessed, from her tone, had been her experience. "Well, that's your decision to make, isn't it?"

"You'd think so," she'd said, a little dubiously.

He'd popped the last bite of cone into his mouth. "Are you ready to head back?"

She'd nodded and picked up her mostly empty ice cream container to drop it into the trash on their way out.

He'd walked her to her car, parked only a few spots away from his truck.

"I know you're not looking forward to the fallout, but you should tell your family," he'd encouraged her. "With two babies on the way, you're going to need not just their support but their help."

"You're right," she'd acknowledged. "I just wish…"

"What?"

She'd sighed and shaken her head. "Nothing."

"You shouldn't waste a wish on nothing," he'd chided gently.

And her lips had curved, just a little.

"What do you wish?" he'd asked again.

"You've already done so much for me," she'd said.

"Tell me what you need. I'll help you if I can."

Because he was apparently a sucker for a damsel in distress—or maybe it was just that he hated to see *this* damsel in distress, as he seemed unable to refuse her anything.

"Will you go with me…to tell my parents?"

Of course, he'd said "yes."

And ten days later, he'd said, "I do."

Chapter Five

He didn't feel any different. But as Connor drove back to Haven, the platinum band on the third finger of his left hand was visible evidence of his newly married status—and proof that everything was about to change.

"You've hardly spoken since we left the chapel," he remarked, with a glance at his wife, sitting silently beside him, her hands folded in her lap. "Having second thoughts already?"

"Are you having them, too?" Regan asked, sounding worried.

"Actually, I'm not. I mean, there were a few moments during the drive when I wondered if we were making a mistake—or at least being too hasty," he acknowledged.

But there were time constraints to their situation that had required quick action—not just because a twin pregnancy would likely show sooner than a single pregnancy but because of the deal he'd made with his now father-in-law.

He'd experienced a moment of hesitation after the legalities were done and the officiant invited Connor to kiss his bride. But it was just a simple kiss. Except that her soft lips had trembled as he brushed them with his own, and her breath had caught in her throat as her eyes lifted to meet his. In that moment, something had passed between them.

Or maybe Connor had just imagined it.

In any event, that moment was gone.

"But I have no doubt that we've done the right thing for your babies," he said to her then.

"What about us?" she'd wondered aloud.

"We'll make it work," he promised.

She twisted her rings around on her finger. "I never even asked if you had a girlfriend."

"Not anymore."

She gasped. "Ohmygod—"

"I'm kidding," he said.

"Oh." She blew out a breath. "For the record, not funny."

"Sorry."

"So…" she began, after another minute had passed in silence. "Why don't you have a girlfriend?"

"I'm not sure my wife would approve," he remarked dryly.

"Also not funny," she told him.

"I've had girlfriends," he'd assured her. "In fact, I dated Courtney Morgan on and off for several months earlier this year."

"What caused the off?"

He shrugged. "We had some good times together, but I think we both knew it was never going to be anything more than that."

"How do you think she'll react to the news of your marriage?" Regan wondered.

"Probably with disbelief, because I told her right from the beginning that I wasn't in any hurry to settle down." And that had been the honest truth at the time, but a lot of things had changed since his first date with Courtney Morgan.

"I think people will be less surprised by the news of our wedding when they realize I'm pregnant," she acknowledged, splaying a hand over her belly. "And with two babies in there, that probably won't be too long."

"There's going to be a lot of gossip," he acknowledged, reaching across the console to take her hand. "But we'll face it together."

But first they had to face her parents.

"I feel a little guilty," he'd admitted, when he pulled his truck into the stamped concrete drive of 1202 Miners' Pass.

"Why?"

"Because you're leaving all of this to come and live with me in a house that's only a fraction of its size."

"Your house is more than adequate," she said. "Although I wouldn't object if you wanted to update the kitchen. In fact, I encourage you to do so."

He opened the passenger-side door and offered his hand to her. "When you start cooking, I'll start thinking about renovating," he said teasingly.

"Just because I don't cook doesn't mean that I can't," she warned. "Celeste taught all of us to make a few basic dishes."

"Suddenly married life is looking a whole lot brighter."

She smiled, but the way she clutched his hand as they made their way to the door told him that she was uneasy anticipating her parents' reactions to the news of their impromptu nuptials.

He wished he could have reassured her that her father, at least, wouldn't object to their marriage. But before he'd exchanged vows with his bride, he'd made a promise to Ben Channing, and he knew that reneging on that promise could jeopardize everything.

As Connor listened to the quiet even breaths of his wife beside him, he knew that was as true now as it had been the day they'd married.

But now, he had so much more to lose.

* * *

Regan hadn't been asleep for long when soft plaintive cries penetrated the hazy fog of her slumber.

Immediately, she felt a tightness in her breasts that she'd started to recognize as the letdown reflex, readying her milk for the babies—because when one was awake and hungry, the other was soon to follow. She sat up, swinging her legs over the side of the mattress and reaching for the hungry infant.

Connor had plugged a night-light into the wall so that she wouldn't have to stumble around in the dark, and as she reached into the bassinet, her heart plummeted to discover there was only one swaddled baby inside.

She gasped and turned her head, searching for her husband in the dimly lit room.

"I'm right here," Connor said. His tone was quiet and reassuring, though the words emanated not from the bed but the rocking chair in the corner. "And Poppy's here, too."

She exhaled a shuddery sigh of relief as she reached into the hidden opening of her nursing gown to unhook the cup of her bra and set Piper to her breast. The baby, hungry and intent, immediately latched on to her nipple and began to suckle. Regan tried not to wince as she settled back on the mattress with the infant tucked in the crook of her arm.

"What are you doing up?" she asked. "Did Poppy wake you?"

"I wasn't really sleeping," he said. "So when she started fussing, I decided to change her diaper and sit with her for a little while in the hope that you'd be able to get a few more minutes' sleep."

"Did I?" she wondered.

"A very few," he told her.

But she was grateful for his effort. "What did I do to deserve a guy like you?" she teased in a whisper.

He rose from the chair and returned to the bed, sitting on top of the covers beside his wife, with Poppy still in his arms. "I'm the lucky one," he said. "I've got a beautiful wife and two gorgeous daughters."

She smiled to lighten the mood, because his tone—and words—had been more serious than she'd expected. "You mean a hormonal wife and two demanding babies?"

He tipped her chin up, forcing her to meet his gaze. "I say what I mean."

"No regrets?" she asked, then held her breath, waiting for his reply.

"Not for me," he immediately replied. "You?"

She shook her head. "Fears, worries and concerns—yes. Regrets—no."

Poppy started to squirm and fuss then, and he shifted her in his arms, offering his finger for her to suck on. That satisfied the infant for all of about ten seconds—until she realized no sustenance was coming out of the digit.

"I guess she's hungry, too," Regan remarked.

"She can wait a few minutes until her sister's finished. Or I could go downstairs and make up a bottle," Connor offered.

She shook her head again as she eased Piper's mouth from her breast and lifted the baby to her shoulder. "Switching back and forth between breast and bottle can cause nipple confusion."

"*Can* doesn't mean *will*," he pointed out.

Piper let out a surprisingly loud burp, then sighed and laid her head down on her mother's shoulder, her eyes already starting to drift shut.

Regan touched her lips to the infant's forehead, then exchanged babies with Connor.

He carried Piper to the dresser and laid her down on the change pad. There was an actual change table in the twins' bedroom, but while they were sleeping in here, it made sense to change them in here, too.

"Everybody talks about how natural breastfeeding is," she said, as she unfastened the other cup of her nursing bra for Poppy. "But that doesn't mean it's easy."

"It's also a personal choice," Connor said. "So you don't have to continue with it if you don't want to."

"I want to," she insisted. "I just worry that I'm not going to be any good at it."

"The lactation consultant at the hospital said you were doing just fine," he reminded her.

"But they seem to be eating all the time," she lamented. "They're eating all the time, and it's only day eight and…"

"And what?" he prompted.

A single tear slid down her cheek. "What if I can't do this?"

Regan's voice was barely a whisper in the quiet room, as if she was afraid to say the words aloud because that might make them true.

"Do what?" Connor asked gently.

Over the past few months, he'd learned that her fears and insecurities, though not unique, were real, and he tried to offer sincere support rather than empty platitudes.

"Feed my babies," she admitted. "What if my body doesn't make enough milk?"

She was his wife. He shouldn't feel uncomfortable having this kind of conversation with her. But theirs wasn't a traditional relationship in which they'd fallen in love after dating for a while. In fact, they'd never been on a date and had only married because she was pregnant and didn't want her babies to grow up without a father, so he didn't think any of the usual rules applied.

He plucked a tissue from the box beside the bed and gently blotted the moisture on her cheek. "The more they take, the more you'll make," he said, echoing the doctor's words. "But if you don't think they're getting enough, it's okay to supplement with formula."

"But Dr. Amaro said that breast is best."

He wished they were talking about something—*anything*—else.

Yes, breastfeeding was natural and normal, and maybe most guys could watch their wives nurse their babies and view it as a simple biological function, but Connor wasn't one of those guys.

He averted his gaze from the creamy swell of her breast and cleared his throat. "And nursing Piper at midnight while Poppy has a bottle is okay, because you'll nurse Poppy at three a.m. and give Piper a bottle then," he suggested reasonably.

"I'd feel like a failure," she admitted.

"You're not a failure," he assured her.

Another tear slid down her cheek. "My nipples hurt."

He really did *not* want to be thinking about her nipples. Or any other part of her anatomy that identified her as female, because his body, too long deprived of sex, couldn't help but respond to her nearness.

Maybe it was inappropriate, but it was undeniable.

He cleared his throat and tried to clear his mind. "Did you try the cream they gave you at the hospital?"

She shook her head.

"Why not?"

"Because—" she sniffled "—I forgot."

He laid the now-sleeping Piper down in her bassinet

and rummaged through the various pockets of the diaper bag until he found the sample size tube of pure lanolin that the doctor had assured them was safe for both mom and babies.

He set it on the bedside table, then picked up her empty water glass. "Do you want a refill?"

"If you don't mind," she said.

He took the glass, grateful for the excuse to escape the room so that he didn't have to attempt to avert his gaze while she rubbed cream on her breasts.

He stepped through the door—and muttered a curse under his breath as he nearly tripped over Baxter.

"What are you doing up here?" he demanded in a whisper.

The dog lifted his head and thumped his tail a few times.

Connor sighed and squatted down to rub the animal's head. "Yes, you're a good boy," he said. "But you're supposed to sleep on *your* bed in the living room, not outside *my* bedroom."

Baxter rose slowly to his feet and stretched.

"Living room," he said again, and pointed toward the stairs.

The dog looked at the stairs, then back to the bedroom again.

"The babies are fine," he promised.

Apparently Baxter was persuaded, because as Connor headed to the kitchen, the dog trotted down the stairs beside him.

"Can I help you find something?" Connor asked, when he returned from his morning walk with Baxter to see his sister-in-law digging through the cupboards in the kitchen.

"Coffee?" Brielle said hopefully.

He pointed to the half-full carafe on the warmer.

She shook her head. "No, I mean *real* coffee."

"Sorry," he said. "I switched to decaf when Regan did."

His sister-in-law frowned. "She doesn't like decaf."

"And therefore isn't tempted to sneak an extra cup," he pointed out.

"I couldn't finish a first cup," she said. "How do you survive on that?" She immediately realized the answer to her own question. "You get the real stuff at the sheriff's office, don't you?"

"Of course," he agreed. "You want to come in for a cup?"

"Desperately," she said, as she plugged in the kettle—and remembered to flip the switch this time. "But I'll settle for herbal tea and try to pretend my body isn't going through serious caffeine withdrawal."

"Have a cookie," he said, nudging the bakery box toward her.

She opened the lid and frowned. "There's only one left—I can't take the last one."

"I took two up to Regan earlier," he said.

"In that case—" she snatched up the cookie and bit into it. "It's not a cup of freshly brewed dark roast, but the sugar rush might give my system a boost."

"Did the babies wake you up in the night?" Connor asked, as he refilled his own mug.

Brie shook her head. "No, I'm a pretty heavy sleeper. But my body's still on Eastern Standard Time, so I've been up since three o'clock."

He'd been up at 3 a.m., too, but then he'd crashed again—at least for a little while. He'd never realized he could enjoy sharing a bed with someone solely for the purpose of sleep, but when he'd managed to tamp down on his inappropriate desire for his wife, he'd found himself comforted by her presence. If their circumstances had been different, he might have shifted closer and wrapped his arms around her. But their circumstances weren't different, so he'd stayed on his own side and only dreamed of breaching the distance between them.

"And by the time you get used to the time change, you'll be heading back to New York," he remarked to his sister-in-law now.

"Most likely," she agreed, as she poured the boiling water into her mug.

Regan wandered into the kitchen then, tightening the belt of her robe around her waist, and her sister pulled another mug out of the cupboard, dropped a tea bag inside, and filled it with water, too.

Brie pushed the mug across the counter. "Are the babies still sleeping?" she asked.

"Not still, just," Regan said, reaching for the tea. "They just went down for a nap. Hopefully, a long one." She lifted a hand to stifle a yawn. "You didn't hear them in the night?"

Brie shook her head. "How many times were they up?"

Regan looked at Connor.

He shrugged. "I lost count."

"Me, too," she admitted. "But I'm pretty sure one or the other was up...almost constantly."

"That sounds about right," he agreed. "And that's why you should go back to bed."

She looked him over, noting the uniform he wore. "I should go back to bed but you're going in to work?"

"I'd be going back to bed, too, if I had the option."

"Which is why you shouldn't have been up with me, every single time, in the night," she pointed out to him.

"I'm fine," he said. "And everyone else will be, too, so long as I don't have to pull out my weapon today."

"You're kidding—I hope."

He chuckled softly. "I'm kidding. And I'm going to pick up dinner on the way home, so you don't have to worry about anything but taking care of the babies and hanging out with your sister today."

"Didn't you say the freezer is full of casseroles from friends and neighbors?" Regan asked.

"It is," he confirmed. "But you mentioned that you've been craving Jo's Pizza."

"I did." She closed her eyes, as if picturing a pie with golden crust and melted cheese, and hummed approvingly. "And I am."

"Then Jo's Pizza it is." He bent down to give Baxter a scratch and started toward the door, then paused and turned back to kiss the top of Regan's head and wave to his sister-in-law before heading out.

"That's a good man you've got there," Brielle said to her sister when Connor had gone.

"He is," Regan agreed, lifting her mug to her lips.

"And yet…" Brie let the words trail off.

She sipped her tea, refusing to take the bait.

Her sister popped the last bite of cookie into her mouth and chewed.

Regan lasted another half a minute before she let out an exasperated sigh and finally asked, "And yet *what*?"

"That's what I'm trying to figure out," Brielle admitted.

"Well, let me know when you do."

"I know I've been gone a long time," Brie acknowledged. "But I know you, Regan. I know how you respond to men you like, and to men you *really* like. And I know there's more—or maybe less—going on here than you want everyone to believe."

"What are you talking about?" she asked.

"I'm talking about your relationship with your husband."

"Connor's amazing," Regan said. Because it was true—but it wasn't the whole truth, and she felt a little guilty that she wasn't being completely honest with her sister. "Since I told him that I was pregnant, he's been there for me. He rearranged his schedule to be at my first ultrasound appointment, and he even went with me to tell Mom and Dad that I was pregnant."

Brie's brows lifted. "*Before* he put a ring on your finger? He's even braver than I would have guessed. But I'm still missing something," she decided. "I'm adding two plus two and somehow only coming up with three."

"You were never particularly good at math," she teased her sister.

"That's why I'm the kindergarten teacher and you're the accountant," Brie agreed. "But as a teacher, I've become adept at knowing when one of my students is hiding something from me, and I know you're hiding something now."

"You're right," Regan acknowledged, almost relieved to say the words aloud, to confide in her sister. "There's something I haven't told you. Something nobody knows."

Brie laid a hand on her sister's arm, a silent gesture of support and encouragement.

"Connor married me because I was pregnant…but he didn't get me pregnant."

Chapter Six

Connor could empathize with his sister-in-law's craving for caffeine, and the always-fresh pot of coffee was his prime target when he arrived at the sheriff's office a short while later.

"I want to see pictures," Judy Talon, the sheriff's administrative assistant, demanded as soon as he walked through the door.

"I've got pictures," he promised. "But I want coffee first."

"Black?" Judy asked, rising from her chair.

When Connor had first been hired, the older woman had clearly and unequivocally stated that she was nobody's secretary or servant. While she had no objection to making coffee, she wasn't going to serve it to anyone else. And in four years, this was the first time she'd ever offered to pour him a cup.

He nodded gratefully. "That would be perfect. Thanks."

Along with the mug of steaming coffee, she brought him a glazed twist from the box of donuts that Deputy Holly Kowalski habitually brought in on Friday mornings.

"Thanks," Connor said again.

"You look like you've had a long day already and it's not yet nine a.m.," she noted.

"Long night," he clarified.

"One of the joys of being a new parent," Judy remarked.

"But these are the real joys," he said, unlocking the screen of his phone to show her the promised photos.

"Oh, they are precious," she agreed, leaning closer for a better look. "And so tiny."

He pointed to the baby with a striped pink cap on her head. "Piper was born at 3:08 a.m., weighing five pounds, eight ounces and measuring eighteen and a half inches." His finger shifted to indicate the baby wearing the dotted pink cap. "Poppy followed fourteen minutes later at five pounds, ten ounces and eighteen inches."

"Piper and Poppy are rather unusual names," Judy remarked.

"Unique," Connor agreed. "Although we did opt for more traditional middle names. Piper's is Faith and Poppy's is Margaret."

"Oh." Judy's lips curved as she glanced down at the phone again. "Your mom would be tickled pink to know that you shared her name with your firstborn."

The sheriff's admin had known his mom "way back when." They hadn't been friends, but Judy had been friendly to Faith, which was more than could be said about a lot of other women in town. They'd attended the same church—that is, his mom had attended when she wasn't required to work on a Sunday morning—and Connor knew there had been occasions when Judy had encouraged Faith to take her kids and leave her deadbeat husband. But Faith Parrish always replied that she'd promised to stick by Dwayne "for better or for worse," and she intended to honor those vows.

"She'd also be so proud of the man you've become," Judy told him now.

"Look at this one," he said, swiping the screen to show

the next photo—hopefully making it clear that he didn't want to talk about his mom.

Faith had been gone for almost five years now. The doctors had ruled her death an accidental overdose, suggesting that her mind had been muddled by the tumor growing on her brain, which resulted in her taking too many pills. Connor had a different theory. He'd overheard his mom talking to a neighbor about her grim prognosis and confiding that she didn't want her sons to watch her waste away. Six weeks later—ten days after Deacon's high school graduation—she was gone.

Connor still missed her every day. He missed her gentle smile and her wise counsel. No doubt she would have something to say about the predicament he'd gotten himself into, but he couldn't begin to imagine what that *something* might be.

Judy continued to *ooh* and *ahh* as she scrolled through the pictures. "Is that Regan—in the hospital?"

He glanced at the screen. "Yeah."

"She looks like someone who just went for a leisurely walk in the park, not someone who just gave birth to two babies."

"She was a trouper," Connor said, flexing the hand that had been clamped by her iron grip with each contraction. "But it was not a walk in the park."

"Says the man whose most strenuous task was probably cutting the cords," Judy said.

"I did cut the cords," he confirmed.

He'd been surprised when Regan asked him if he wanted to perform the task—and even more surprised to discover that he did. And still, he hadn't been prepared for the significance of the moment or how severing the tangible link between mother and child somehow seemed to forge a stronger bond connecting all of them.

"My husband did it when our son was born," Judy told him. "But he was in Afghanistan when our daughter was born. She's twenty-four now and regularly gripes that she's still waiting for him to cut the cord."

"Or maybe it's just hard for dads to let go of their little girls—even when they're not so little anymore," Connor said.

"That's probably true, too," she acknowledged. "And lucky for you that you have a badge and gun, because if those girls grow up to be as pretty as their mama, you're going to need both to keep the boys at bay."

"Don't I know it," he agreed.

"Hey, look who's back," Holly said, coming up from the evidence storage locker downstairs. "Congratulations, Deputy Daddy." She went to her desk to retrieve an oversize gift bag, then set it on top of his.

"What's this?" He eyed the package suspiciously.

She chuckled. "It's going to be fun watching you raise two little girls if just the sight of pink tissue makes you cower with fear."

"I'm not afraid," he denied. "I'm just...surprised."

"Surprised that I'd give a gift to my coworker's new babies?" she prompted, sounding hurt.

"Yes. I mean, no. I—"

"Why don't you shut up and open the gift?" Judy suggested.

Deciding that was good advice, Connor pulled out the tissue that was stuffed in the top of the bag and then two neatly folded blankets. He opened up the first, noted the patchwork of pale pinks and soft purples. The second blanket was a different pattern in the same colors. "Thanks, Kowalski. We can definitely use more blankets."

Judy shook her head despairingly. "Those aren't baby

blankets. They're handmade quilts. That one—" she nodded to the one that Connor was holding "—I recognize as a pinwheel pattern. But this one—" she traced a fingertip over a line of tiny stitches and glanced questioningly at Holly.

"That's a fractured star," she said.

"It's beautiful," the admin told her. "They both are. I especially love how you used the same fabrics in the different patterns so that the quilts coordinate."

Connor frowned and turned his attention back to the deputy. "You *made* these?"

"Kowalski's more than just a deadeye with her service pistol," Sheriff Reid Davidson remarked, as he entered the bullpen.

"Apparently," Connor agreed.

"Tessa won't go to sleep without the one you made for her," Reid told Holly.

She actually blushed in response to his praise. "I'm glad she likes it."

The sheriff shifted his gaze to encompass the other deputy and his admin. "And if you were going to have a baby shower in the office, you should have invited the boss."

"Your invitation must have gotten lost in the mail," Judy retorted.

"I'm sure it did," he remarked, his tone dry.

Connor folded the blankets—*quilts*—and put them back in the bag.

"You could have taken a few more days, Neal," Reid said.

"Regan's got her sister helping her out today, so I figured I'd come in and try to catch up on some paperwork."

The sheriff nodded as he filled his mug with coffee.

"Are you ready for your Stranger Danger presentation at the elementary school, Kowalski?"

"Is that today?" The female deputy feigned surprise. "Because I have a dentist appoint—"

"You don't have a dentist appointment," her boss interrupted. "Or if you do, you're going to cancel it, because this has been on your calendar since the beginning of the month."

She sighed. "Maybe you should send Neal," she suggested. "You don't want to depend on a sleep-deprived new dad to back you up if you have to take down a strung-out junkie."

The sheriff shook his head. "You're the only person I know who'd rather face a strung-out junkie than a room full of second-graders."

"Because no one would fault me for shooting the junkie," she pointed out.

"Stoney Ridge Elementary School. Eleven o'clock," Reid said. "And Kowalski?"

"Yes, sir?"

"Lock up your weapon before you go."

Connor coughed to cover up his laugh.

The sheriff lifted the lid of the donut box. "Dammit— who took my glazed twist?"

Kowalski didn't even try to disguise her snicker.

Regan held her breath in anticipation of Brie's response to her confession about the paternity of her twin babies.

"Wait a minute." Her sister held up a hand, apparently needing another moment to process the startling revelation. "Are you telling me that your husband isn't Piper and Poppy's father?"

"He's their father in every way that counts," Regan insisted. "They just don't share his DNA."

"Does he know?" Brie asked cautiously.

"Of course he knows," she said.

Her sister seemed relieved by her response, albeit still a little puzzled. "But if he's not the father and he *knows* he's not the father—biologically," she hastened to clarify, "why did he marry you?"

"Because I was a damsel in distress and he has a white knight complex?" Regan suggested.

Brie immediately shook her head. "I've never known a woman more capable of rescuing herself from any situation than you."

"I appreciate the vote of confidence, but you weren't here when I took the home pregnancy test," Regan reminded her. "Or when I finally told Mom and Dad."

But Connor had been—at least on the latter occasion—and she'd repaid his kindness by metaphorically throwing him to the wolves.

She'd taken his advice and told her parents the truth about the pregnancy. Except for one, tiny detail...

"What just happened in there?" he demanded when they left the house on Miners' Pass. "Why did you let your parents think I *was the father of your babies?"*

"Because if they hadn't assumed you were the father, they would have asked a hundred questions about him and our relationship."

"Questions you didn't want to answer," he realized.

"Questions I can't answer." She buried her face in her hands. "Not without admitting that I had an affair with a married man."

"You didn't know he was married," he said, repeating what she'd previously told him.

"But maybe I should have known. Maybe I didn't ask enough questions."

"All of that's academic now," he pointed out.

"I'll tell them the truth," she promised.

"When?" he demanded.

"Soon. I just need some time to figure out what to say."

"Here's a suggestion— 'Connor Neal isn't the father of my babies.'"

But then, before she'd had a chance to right the wrong, he'd apparently had a change of heart. Instead of distancing himself from the mess she'd made of her life, he'd offered to marry her—putting himself squarely in the middle of it.

"I was completely freaking out," Regan confided to her sister now. "I hated lying to Mom and Dad. I was having a really hard time processing the news that I was having twins! And although I wanted to believe that I could be a single mom, Connor's proposal gave me another option. A better option for my babies."

"Still, marriage is a pretty big step to take without any previous investment in the relationship," Brie noted.

Regan nodded. "But Connor grew up without a father—excluding the few years he lived with an abusive stepfather—and he didn't want Piper and Poppy to be subjected to whispers and speculation about their paternity."

"That's admirable," her sister said. "But it implies that he would have offered a ring to any unmarried woman who got knocked up."

"I wasn't any unmarried woman," she pointed out. "I was one who could bolster his standing in the community."

Brie frowned at that. "You're not seriously suggesting that he married you because our mother was a Blake?"

"It was a factor," Regan acknowledged. "Marrying into one of the town's founding families seemed like a surefire way for a man from the wrong side of the tracks to elevate his status in the community."

"He told you that?"

She nodded.

"That seems rather calculating," her sister noted. "On the other hand, it also makes a little more sense to me—a marriage of convenience for both of you."

"Except that it doesn't always feel convenient," Regan confided.

"Because you have feelings for him?" Brie guessed.

"Yes. No." She sighed. "I don't know."

"Well, as long as you're sure," her sister remarked dryly.

"I have all kinds of feelings," she said. "But I don't know if they're feelings *for* Connor or if the overwhelming love I feel for my babies is spilling over in his direction. Or maybe I'm just so grateful to him for everything he's done that I'm making something out of nothing."

"You could also be transferring your feelings for the biological father to the man who stepped up to take his place," her sister suggested as another alternative.

This time Regan shook her head. "I wasn't in love with Bo Larsen."

"So how did you end up in bed with him?" Brie wondered.

"He was handsome and charming, and it had been a really long time since a handsome and charming man showed any interest in me."

"Does he know...that you had his babies?"

"No," she admitted. "I mean, I told him that I was pregnant, because I thought that was the right thing to do."

"How did he respond?"

"He gave me money for an abortion."

Brie responded to that with a single word that questioned *his* paternity, and the fierceness of her response made Regan smile.

"I haven't seen or spoken to him since," she said.

"I assume that means he isn't from Haven?"

"No, he's not," she confirmed. "He was in town for a few months on a business contract, and when the contract ended he went back to Logan City—and his wife."

Brie's eyes went wide. "He was *married*?"

Regan felt her cheeks burn with a hot combination of guilt and remorse. "*Is* married," she corrected. "Though I had no idea, when we were together, that he had a wife." She swallowed. "And…two daughters."

"Wow."

She nodded, her face flaming with the memory of their confrontation—and her shame upon hearing his revelation.

"When did you find out?" her sister asked.

"When I told him that I was pregnant. Until then…I had no idea *I* was the other woman."

"Oh, honey." Brie wrapped warm, comforting arms around her. "I'm so sorry."

"I was such a fool," Regan noted.

"We all make mistakes when it comes to matters of the heart," her sister said. "And occasionally an overload of hormones."

She managed to smile through her tears. "You're the only one, besides Connor, who knows the whole truth."

"My lips are sealed," her sister promised. "But I have to admit, I'm curious about something."

"What's that?"

"Your platonic relationship with your husband."

The comment blipped on Regan's radar. She knew Brielle too well to assume this was an innocent question. "Why is that curious?" she asked, unwilling to admit that she was less-than-thrilled that Connor seemed determined not to stray beyond the friend zone. She should focus on what they had rather than wishing for more.

"Because it's obvious to me that there's some real chemistry between the two of you—and equally obvious that you're both pretending to be unaware of it."

"The only thing obvious to me is that your romantic heart is looking for a happy ending where one doesn't exist," Regan said.

But there was a part of her that wished her sister was right—and a happy ending wasn't outside the realm of possibility.

Chapter Seven

Connor hadn't thought to ask Brielle what she liked on her pizza, so he ordered two pies: one with bacon, pineapple and black olives—Regan's favorite, and one with only pepperoni. Of course, when he went into Jo's to pick up the order, he had to pull out his phone again and show pictures of the babies to everyone gathered around the counter.

Not that he minded—especially when Jo refused to take his money "just this once," suggesting that he should put it into a college fund for his daughters, because it was never too early to start saving. He knew that she was speaking the truth. He also knew that, even if he started saving right now, the spare pennies from a deputy's salary wouldn't add up to enough.

Thankfully, Piper and Poppy's maternal grandparents had expressed their intention to set up education funds for both of them, as they'd already done for their other granddaughter. He wanted to resent all the ways that the Channings threw their money around, but that would be rather hypocritical considering how he'd already benefited from their generosity.

When he finally got home, he found his wife and her sister snuggling with the babies in the living room. Baxter usually raced to the door whenever he heard Connor's truck pull into the driveway, but today the dog didn't move from his sentry position on the floor in front of the sofa.

"So much for man's best friend," he lamented, though he didn't really object to the dog's allegiance to the newest members of the family.

Baxter lifted his head to sniff the air—or, more likely, the pizza—then gave a soft *woof*.

He set the flat boxes on the coffee table and the dog rose to his feet, his nose twitching.

"Not for you."

Baxter looked at his master, pleading in his big brown eyes.

"He's had his dinner," Regan said. "So don't let him tell you any differently."

The animal swung his head to look at her, a wordless reproach.

"Well, you have," Regan said to him, as she rose to her feet to lay Poppy down in the playpen. "And you're not allowed people food, anyway."

Baxter let out a sound remarkably like a sigh and dropped to the floor again, his chin on top of his paws.

Connor went to the kitchen to get plates and napkins. When he returned, he saw that his sister-in-law hadn't moved from her position on the sofa.

"It will be easier to hold a plate without a baby in your arms," he remarked.

"Probably," Brielle agreed. "But I don't think I'm ready to let this little one go."

"Your nieces will still be here long after the pizza is gone," Regan pointed out, as she lifted a gooey slice covered with bacon, pineapple and olives onto her plate.

"A valid point," her sister acknowledged, and laid Piper down beside her twin.

"By the way, you can probably skip the w-a-l-k to-night," Regan said to Connor, as he loaded up his plate.

"Why's that?" he asked.

"We took him—and the babies—out this afternoon."

He frowned. "The wind was a little brisk this after-noon."

"It didn't seem to bother him," his wife remarked.

"I was thinking about Piper and Poppy," he clarified.

"They were wearing hats and mitts and tucked under a blanket in their stroller—even Mrs. Lopez approved," Regan assured him.

"I'll bet she was thrilled to get a peek at them."

"And Baxter was in doggy heaven because she kept slipping him treats while we were chatting."

"So you did the long route," he realized.

"And then some," Regan agreed. "Brie didn't believe me that the old Stagecoach Inn had reopened, so we went by there, too."

"It's been open a few months now, I think," Connor said.

"Since Valentine's Day, according to the brochure I picked up and which promises the ultimate romantic ex-perience any day of the year," his sister-in-law noted.

"Well, Liam Gilmore's investment certainly seems to be paying off, because there are always cars in the parking lot."

Brie went still, then slowly turned and looked at her sister. "You didn't mention that Liam Gilmore owned the hotel."

"I didn't think it mattered," Regan said.

"It doesn't," Brie said, but the sudden flatness in her tone suggested otherwise.

Connor knew about the acrimonious history between the Blakes and the Gilmores, of course, but he sensed that his sister-in-law's reaction was based on something more recent.

"People rave about The Home Station restaurant, too," he said, in an effort to defuse the sudden tension.

"Have you eaten there?" Brie asked him.

He shook his head. "It's impossible to get a table without a reservation, and reservations aren't easy to get."

"That's hardly surprising. When I lived here, the only place you could go for a decent meal in this town was Diggers'. Or Jo's, if you wanted pizza," she added. "Which, by the way, was delicious."

"And now, instead of going to Battle Mountain for a special occasion, people from Battle Mountain are coming here to celebrate," Regan told her.

"And I thought nothing had changed in the seven years I was gone," Brie remarked lightly.

"For six of those years, nothing did," her sister agreed.

"But now I have a brother-in-law and two adorable nieces—and a pedicure appointment at Serenity Spa with my sister tomorrow afternoon."

"Really?" Regan was obviously surprised by this announcement.

"Two o'clock," Brie confirmed.

His wife sighed happily. "I haven't had a pedicure in…a very long time. Then again, for a very long time, I couldn't even see my feet, so pampering them seemed unnecessary."

"Pampering isn't ever necessary but it's always fun," her sister said. "And after our treatments, I'm going to take a closer look at the hotel, because it looks like the perfect place for a romantic getaway for new parents who never had a honeymoon."

It didn't require much reading between the lines to realize that Brie was thinking about her sister and brother-in-law.

Connor exchanged an uneasy glance with his wife before she looked away again, her cheeks flushed with color. Because she didn't want to imagine a romantic getaway with her husband? he wondered.

Or because she did?

They had their pedicures Saturday afternoon, then Brielle insisted on cooking dinner for her sister and brother-in-law Saturday night. The chicken simmered in a white wine sauce was tender and delicious—one of Celeste's recipes, Brie confided. After dinner the sisters stayed up late talking, trying to squeeze every possible minute out of a visit that was soon coming to an end.

On Sunday they went to Regan's parents' house for brunch, so that the whole family could celebrate the twins' birth together before Brie headed back to New York City.

Connor wouldn't have minded skipping the event. He always felt a little out of step around his in-laws—or maybe it was just that he didn't have a lot of experience with such family get-togethers. But he wanted Piper and Poppy to grow up with a strong sense of family and the security of belonging, so he tamped down on his own discomfort and carried the babies' car seats out to the truck.

It would be a tight squeeze for Brie in the backseat between the two babies, but it wasn't a long drive. Of course, nothing in Haven was too far from anything else, although the town was starting to expand and push out its long-established boundaries. The Channings' house—three towering stories of stone and brick—was an architectural masterpiece in the newest residential development. To a man who'd grown up in very modest circumstances, it was more than impressive—it was intimidating.

Connor pulled into the concrete drive behind a truck that he recognized as belonging to Regan's younger brother Spencer, a former bull rider turned horse trainer. The truck parked in front of Spencer's had the Adventure Village logo painted on the driver's side door, confirming that it belonged to Regan's older brother Jason, who owned the family-friendly recreational facilities. Jason was married to Alyssa—a West Coast native who, for reasons that no one could fathom, had willingly traded in the sun and surf of Southern California for the arid mountains of Northern Nevada.

"Looks like everyone's here," Brie remarked, sounding relieved as she lifted the twins' diaper bag onto her shoulder.

"I don't see Gramps's truck," Regan noted.

"Maybe he decided to stay at the ranch to watch over the cows."

Again, Connor suspected there was a deeper meaning to her words. Although Jesse Blake continued to supervise operations at Crooked Creek Ranch, the modest herd was more of a hobby than a livelihood now that the family's focus had shifted to mining.

Though Regan had lived in the fancy house on Miners' Pass prior to her marriage to Connor, she rang the bell and waited for the door to be opened rather than just walking in. And while he'd become accustomed to the formality—unheard of at his mother's house—it still gave him a start when the door was opened by a uniformed housekeeper.

Apparently it wasn't hard to find good help if you were able to pay for it, he mused, as Greta took their coats. And Ben and Margaret could definitely afford it.

If the Channings hadn't been filthy rich, they likely would have been viewed as neglectful parents. Because they owned and operated the mines that kept half the town employed, excuses were readily made for the parents who were simply too busy to attend teacher conferences, holiday plays, awards ceremonies and—in Spencer's case—even high school graduation.

If Ben and Margaret harbored any regrets about the milestone events they'd missed sharing with Jason, Regan, Spencer and Brielle, they never said as much. But it appeared to Connor that his in-laws were making a distinct effort to be involved in the lives of their grandchildren more than they'd ever done for their children.

They'd surprised Dani with the gift of a pony for her fourth birthday—and surprised Dani's father even more by actually attending the party rather than just sending the gift with their regrets. When Piper and Poppy were born, the maternal grandparents weren't the first visitors to the hospital—Alyssa and Jason took that honor—but they did show up on the first day. And now they'd cleared their schedules—because yes, even on a Sunday, their time was in demand—to host a family gathering where everyone could coo over and cuddle the newest additions to the family. (Though Connor noticed that his mother-in-law seemed more comfortable with cooing than cuddling.)

Of course, it was Celeste who'd done the real work. The Channings' longtime housekeeper and cook—solely responsible for planning and preparing meals since her employers had moved into a much bigger house—had prepared a veritable feast for the occasion, with breakfast items such as eggs benedict, bacon, sausage and pancakes. She'd also baked a ham, made cheesy scalloped potatoes, a green bean casserole and cornbread. An apparent new offering on the menu—fruit salad with mini-marshmallows—was a big hit with Dani, though Connor noted that his wife took a second scoop of the salad, too, after she'd polished off her first serving.

She'd frequently lamented the extra twelve pounds she still carried after giving birth—and that she was always hungry. The doctor had assured her that was normal for a nursing mom—and she was nursing two babies!

Connor didn't know how to reassure her that she looked great, because he didn't want to focus on how great she looked. He didn't want to acknowledge that he was wildly attracted to his wife or that he thought those new curves looked really good on her. Or maybe it was motherhood that added a softness to her features and a glow to her cheeks.

Conversation during the meal touched on numerous and various topics: Jason and Alyssa's recent trip to California over the spring break; the surprise visit of a famous actor to Crooked Creek with a request for Spencer to train his horses; excited recitations of Dani's riding lessons; a discussion of Brie's options for summer employment—because she couldn't imagine doing nothing for the ten weeks of her summer break.

Regan's maternal grandfather—known as Gramps—was in attendance, having driven over from Crooked Creek with Spencer's family, who now lived in the main house on the ranch. Connor noticed that the old man didn't contribute much to the various conversations that took place during the meal, but he kept a close eye on the little girl seated beside him, helping to fill Dani's plate with the foods she wanted, even cutting her pancakes and pouring the maple syrup. Though he hadn't been part of the family for very long, Connor had heard murmurs about a rift between Gramps and his granddaughter visiting from New York City. The lack of any direct inter-action between them gave credence to those murmurs.

"I can't believe you're going back to New York al-ready," Jason said to Brielle, as he dug his fork into his lemon pie. "It seems like you just got here."

"Because she did," Spencer agreed.

"I've been here four days," Brie reminded them.

"Four whole days?" her oldest brother echoed. "You've definitely overstayed your welcome."

"And," she continued, ignoring his sarcasm, "I've got fifteen six-year-olds who will be waiting for me at eight thirty Monday morning."

"Because some people have real jobs," Alyssa teased her husband.

"Just because I don't punch a clock doesn't mean I don't work hard," he replied, a little defensively.

"I know, " she said soothingly.

"On the bright side, I think I've almost convinced Brie to come back in June, for Piper and Poppy's baptism," Regan announced.

"Really?" Margaret looked at her youngest daughter, her expression equal parts surprised and hopeful.

"So long as it's later in June, after school's finished," Brie said.

"We'll make it late June," Regan promised.

"And by then it will be time to look at flights for Thanksgiving," Kenzie said. "Because they tend to book up fast."

Brie shook her head. "I won't be coming back again in November."

"But you have to," her friend and sister-in-law said. "You set a precedent by coming home to meet Piper and Poppy, so it's only fair that you do the same for your next niece or nephew."

The silence that fell around the table was broken by Spencer's four-and-a-half-year-old daughter. "Can I say it now?" Dani asked. "Can I?"

Spencer put a finger to his lips, urging her to shush. "We're going to give Auntie Brie—and everyone else—another minute to figure it out."

The little girl crossed her arms over her chest, clearly unhappy with this decision. "But you said that *I* could tell everyone about our baby," she reminded him, obviously in protest of the change of plans.

"And you just did," Gramps remarked, evidently amused enough by the exchange to speak up.

At the same time Brie put the pieces together and said to Kenzie, "You're pregnant?"

Spencer's wife nodded, the wide smile that spread across her face further confirmation of the happy news. "Our family will be growing by one in early November."

"Or maybe we can have two babies, like Auntie Regan," Dani chimed in hopefully.

Connor and Regan shared a look, silently communicating amusement that anyone would wish for the double duty that came with twin babies—and a wordless acknowledgment that they'd been doubly blessed by the arrival of Piper and Poppy.

"We're *not* having two babies," her stepmother said firmly.

"Not this time, anyway," Spencer said, with a conspiratorial wink for his daughter.

Dani sighed. "Well, can we at least have a girl baby, then?"

"We won't know if we're having a girl or a boy until the baby's born," Kenzie cautioned.

"But the news of another baby—girl *or* boy—is cause for celebration," Ben said.

"And that means we're going to need a bottle of champagne," his wife decided.

"A great idea," Regan remarked dryly. "Let's celebrate Kenzie's pregnancy with alcohol that she can't drink."

"Well, we'll open a bottle of nonalcoholic champagne, too," Margaret said.

Celeste brought in the bottles of bubbly, along with enough champagne glasses for everyone. Corks were popped as best wishes and embraces were shared around the table.

Spencer, in charge of pouring the nonalcoholic bubbly, distributed glasses to his expectant wife, his young daughter and his sister—the nursing mom.

"I'll have a glass of that, please," Alyssa said, gesturing to the bottle in his hand.

"Why? Are you pregnant, too?" Spencer teased his brother's wife.

"Can't a woman decline alcohol without everyone assuming she's pregnant?" Alyssa countered.

"Of course," Regan spoke up in her sister-in-law's defense. "But it's interesting that you avoided answering his question by asking one of your own."

Alyssa, her cheeks flushed, turned to look helplessly at her husband.

"We were planning to wait awhile longer before sharing our news," Jason said. "But yes, we're going to have a baby before the end of this year, too."

"When?" Kenzie immediately wanted to know.

"Late November," Alyssa confided.

Of course, this news was followed by more hugs and congratulations as the rest of the glasses were passed around the table.

"Champagne?" Margaret asked, offering her youngest daughter a glass.

"I definitely want alcohol," Brie replied. "Because I'm beginning to suspect that there's something in the water in this town, and I'm not taking any chances."

Chapter Eight

It was harder than Regan expected to say goodbye to her sister. For the past seven years, she'd had regular if not frequent contact with Brielle via text, email and Face-Time, but visits had been few and far between.

She'd gone to New York a couple of times, but it was different there. Brielle had been pleased to have Regan stay with her and her roommates hadn't voiced any objections—they were happy to include her in all their plans. But that was the problem: they always seemed to have plans, which meant that Regan had little one-on-one time with her sister.

Regan didn't begrudge her sister these friendships. In fact, she genuinely liked Lily and Grace, and she had other friends of her own, too. But none that she was particularly close with or would confide her deepest secrets to.

Had she ever shared that kind of kinship with anyone other than Brielle? Maybe, when she was younger. But once she'd set upon her career path, she'd focused on that to the exclusion of all else. And anyway, there were some secrets that she didn't feel she could entrust to anyone outside the family—such as the truth about Piper and Poppy's paternity.

When Ben and Margaret left to take Brielle to the airport, the rest of the siblings said their goodbyes to one another and went their separate ways. Celeste had packed up various leftovers for each family, instinctively knowing who would want what. Which was why Dani happily skipped out the door with a Tupperware container of marshmallow fruit salad in her hands.

Regan and Connor were the last to leave, taking longer than everyone else who wasn't carting around twin babies. For the new parents, the cook had prepared plates of baked ham, scalloped potatoes and beans that could be easily reheated in the microwave for their dinner.

"Are you sure you don't want to come home with us?" Connor asked as he accepted the plates.

"Don't think I'm not tempted," she told him, her wistful gaze shifting to the twins securely buckled into their matching car seats. "But I promise, anytime you want to bring those babies for a visit, you won't leave here hungry."

Celeste gave an extra hug to the new mom before she left. "You used to spend so much time working, I was afraid you'd never meet and fall in love with a wonderful man," she said quietly, her words for Regan alone. "I'm so glad to see that I was wrong. And so happy to know that he loves you, too."

Regan hugged her back, saying only, "Thank you for everything today."

Because while there was no denying that Connor was a wonderful man, their marriage wasn't the love match that Celeste obviously believed it to be—and that Regan found herself starting to wish it *could* be.

Baxter was waiting at the door, fairly dancing with excitement as he greeted them upon their return. He didn't wait for Connor to put the car seats down, but walked all the way around them, sniffing, his tail wagging happily because his favorite little humans were finally home. When the sleeping babies were transferred from their car seats to the bassinet in the master bedroom, Baxter immediately settled down beside it.

The parents retreated to the living room, where Regan dropped onto the sofa and stretched her legs out in front of her.

"What are your plans for the rest of the day?" Connor asked her.

"To do as little as possible," she admitted.

"Do you mind if I join you?"

She patted the empty space beside her.

"Are you up for a movie?" he asked, reaching for the television remote.

"Put on whatever you want," she said. "Because there's no guarantee I'll stay awake to watch anything."

He grinned. "That means I don't have to worry about picking something you'll like."

She smiled back, grateful and relieved for the easy camaraderie they shared. Maybe this wasn't quite how she'd imagined marriage would be, but she had no cause for complaint.

It had taken some time for them to become comfortable with one another and their new living arrangement, and adjustments had been made on both sides. They shared some common interests, including a love of dogs, action movies, baseball games and Jo's pizza. And they respected their differences with regard to musical preferences, literary genres and art appreciation. Most important, they talked and laughed together, and she knew that he loved Piper and Poppy as much as she did.

And—except for that one time, during the Christmas holiday three months earlier—he seemed completely oblivious to the fact that she was female. Which maybe wasn't something she should complain about, she acknowledged, recalling a conversation she'd overheard between two of her coworkers.

The women had been complaining about the unrealistic expectations of their respective husbands. As if, after working at an office all day and then running around after the kids at home, the wives wanted nothing more than to indulge the sexual fantasies of their partners.

"I might feel a little more energetic in the bedroom if he put a load of laundry in the washing machine while I was making dinner," Becky had said.

Sandra nodded. "Or pulled out the vacuum every once in a while instead of waiting for me to do it."

Regan had listened to their chatter with sympathy but she had nothing to add. Because the truth was, Connor probably did twice as much laundry as she did. He even hung up her delicates, as recommended by the labels, instead of tossing them into the dryer. And if he spilled crumbs on the floor, it was likely that Baxter would clean them up before the vacuum could be plugged in. But when it came to other household chores, he was more than willing to do his share, if not more.

No, she had no cause for complaint, she reminded herself.

Except...wasn't it unusual for a man not to express an interest in sex? Even if there was a lot about their marriage that wasn't usual.

They hadn't specifically discussed sleeping arrangements before their impromptu wedding ceremony, but he'd vacated his bed for her, confirming that physical intimacy wasn't part of their bargain—and maybe not even desired. But if "separate rooms" was a marriage of convenience "rule," she was starting to think they should throw out the rule book.

Of course, she'd already been pregnant when they got

married, and maybe Connor was turned off by the idea of making love with a woman who was carrying another man's baby. Or maybe he just wasn't attracted to her at all—although the passionate kiss they'd shared in December certainly suggested otherwise.

She tipped her head back and closed her eyes as the memory of that kiss played out in her mind and stirred her body.

"You might be more comfortable upstairs, if you want to take a nap," he suggested.

And the tantalizing memory slipped away, leaving only the remnants of an unsatisfied hunger.

Regan held back a regretful sigh as she shook her head. "If I go upstairs, the babies might wake up. It's almost as if they can sense when their food supply is in close proximity."

"You nursed them before we left your parents' place, though, so they should be okay for a while, I'd think."

She held up her hand, showing her fingers were crossed.

And though she tried to hold back a wistful sigh, she must have made some sound because Connor asked, "Are you okay?"

"Yeah," she said, albeit not very convincingly.

"I know you're going to miss your sister, but she's going to come back in a couple of months for the baptism, and probably again in November, after Spencer and Kenzie's baby is born. Or maybe at Christmas, to meet Alyssa and Jason's baby at the same time."

Regan nodded. "I'm sure you're right. And I am going to miss Brie, but…it's more than that," she admitted.

He shifted on the sofa, so that he was facing her, and took her hands in his. "What's more than that?"

Her eyes filled with tears. "Everyone was so happy

to hear the news about Spencer and Kenzie's baby—and then Jason and Alyssa's baby."

"You mean, unlike your parents' reactions when you told them about your pregnancy," he guessed.

She nodded again. "Obviously my situation was different," she acknowledged. "And although I wouldn't change anything that happened, because we've got Piper and Poppy now, I sometimes wish I'd been able to savor the joy of discovering that I was going to be a mother. Instead, I was too busy being worried that I was going to have to do everything on my own."

Connor squeezed her hands gently. "You're not on your own now."

Regan smiled. "I know. And thanks to you, I was able to relax and prepare for the babies during the last five months of my pregnancy."

His brows lifted. "When were you relaxed? Was I out of town that day?"

She elbowed him in the ribs.

He chuckled.

"Seriously, though, I hope you know how grateful I am to you. For everything."

"We entered into a mutually beneficial arrangement," he reminded her.

"It sounds so romantic when you phrase it like that," she said dryly.

He shrugged. "Romance isn't really my thing."

"It was never mine, either." She lifted her head to meet his gaze. "But lately I've found myself wondering if that could change."

Then, before she could think about all the reasons it might be a mistake, she leaned forward and pressed her lips to his.

It wasn't the first, or even the second, time they'd

kissed, but somehow Connor had managed to forget how potent her flavor was. Now her sweet taste raced through his veins like a drug, making his heart hammer and his blood pound. And like an addict coming down from that first euphoric rush, he wanted more.

She sensed his desire, and willingly gave more. She didn't hold anything back. When he touched his tongue to her lip—testing, teasing, she sighed softly and opened for him—readily, eagerly. Her hands slid over his shoulders to link behind his head, her fingers tangling in the hair that brushed the collar of his shirt. The gentle scrape of her nails against his scalp had all the blood draining out of his head and into his lap.

His arms banded around her, pulling her closer. Her breasts, full and plump, were crushed against his chest. Their tongues touched, retreated. Once. Twice. More. The rhythmic dance mimicked the sensual act of lovemaking and somehow made him impossibly harder.

He wanted her—more than he could ever remember wanting another woman. But she wasn't another woman; she was his wife. And not even two weeks had passed since she'd given birth to their twin baby girls. Maybe he didn't share any of their DNA, but his name was in the "father" box on their birth registration. That status not only gave him certain rights and responsibilities, it was a gift that he was trying to prove himself worthy of.

With a muttered curse and sincere regret, he eased his mouth from hers.

Regan exhaled, slowly and a little unsteadily, before lifting her gaze to his. "What's wrong?"

"We got married so that your babies would have a father," he reminded her. "I didn't—*don't*—expect anything more."

He saw a flicker of something—disappointment?

hurt?—in her eyes before she looked away. "Are you seeing someone else?"

"What?" He was shocked that she would even consider such a possibility. "No! Of course not."

"So you're being faithful to a wife you're not even sleeping with?"

"We exchanged vows," he reminded her. "And I don't make promises lightly."

She considered his words for a moment. "I can appreciate that," she said. "But what I really want to know is—are you at all attracted to me?"

Connor was baffled by the question.

How was it possible that she couldn't know how much he wanted her?

But apparently she didn't, and he decided that admitting the truth and intensity of his desire for her might do more harm than good at this point.

"Regardless of my feelings, there are times when it's smarter to ignore an attraction than give in to it," he said.

"Maybe—if you're attracted to your best friend's sister or another man's girlfriend," she allowed. "But I don't think there's any danger in acting on feelings for your own wife."

"Honey, you are the most dangerous woman I've ever known," he assured her. "Not to mention that anything we start here is doomed to remain unfinished."

"There are various ways to finish," she pointed out. Then, in case he needed more convincing, she leaned forward to nibble playfully on his lower lip.

"There are," he agreed hoarsely, and his body was more than ready to accept any variation that she wanted to offer.

This time he reached for her. His hand slid beneath the curtain of her hair to cradle the back of her head, holding her in place while his mouth moved over hers. His kiss was hot and hungry. Desperate and demanding.

Somehow she found herself in his lap, where she could feel the solid evidence of his arousal pressed hard against her, stoking the embers of her own desire. His hands were on her breasts now, gently kneading, his thumbs brushing over her peaked nipples. Even through the lightly padded cups of her nursing bra, she was hyperaware of his touch, as arrows of sensation shot from the tips of her breasts to her core, stirring an unexpectedly urgent hunger.

She arched into him, wanting, *needing*, more. More of his touch. More of his taste. More everything.

She reached between their bodies to unfasten his belt, then released the button of his jeans. The zipper required more effort and attention as the fabric was stretched taut over his straining erection, but she finally succeeded and rewarded herself by sliding her hand beneath the band of his briefs to take hold of her prize.

As her fingers wrapped around him, his groan of approval reverberated through her, encouraging and emboldening her. In the far recesses of her mind, she thought she heard something—maybe a sound coming from the baby monitor? But it was a vague inkling that failed to draw her attention away from her task.

Then Baxter woofed—a sound not so vague or distant.

Regan tried to ignore the dog and concentrate on the task in hand, but Baxter, apparently displeased that she wasn't already racing up the stairs in response to the sounds of a baby stirring, put his paws up on the edge of the sofa and nudged her arm with his nose.

She couldn't help it—she giggled. Her husband cursed. The dog nudged her again, more insistently this time. Connor put his hand over hers, halting her motions.

"You better go check on the babies," he said. "Because Baxter isn't going to give us any peace until you do."

She knew he was right, and she appreciated the animal's diligence—although not as much as she resented the interruption right now. "I'll be quick," she promised.

But the twins conspired to thwart her efforts.

When she reached the bedroom, Poppy was wide awake and demanding attention. Regan changed the baby's diaper, then settled into the rocking chair with the hungry infant at her breast.

Of course, by the time Poppy was sated, Piper was awake, so Regan had to go through the whole routine again. She was fastening a fresh diaper around the infant's middle when Connor popped his head into the room.

"Everything okay?" he asked.

"Yeah, but the girls both decided it was dinner time—again, and I'm just getting started with Piper."

"In that case, I might as well take Baxter out," he said. "He's pacing by the door, eager for his w-a-l-k."

She nodded and returned to the rocking chair to feed her firstborn daughter. When Piper was finished nursing, Regan laid the now-sleepy baby down in the bassinet beside her twin.

Then she stretched out on the bed to eagerly wait for her husband's return...and was fast asleep only minutes later.

Chapter Nine

Connor wasn't surprised to find his wife completely out when he returned home. To be honest, he might even have been relieved to discover that Regan had succumbed to her obvious exhaustion. After all, wasn't that one of the reasons he'd decided to treat Baxter to an extra-long walk?

Well, that, and to give himself the necessary time and distance to cool the heat that pulsed in his veins. Because while she'd given every indication that she craved physical intimacy as much as he did, he worried that he'd taken advantage of her vulnerable state.

She'd been through a lot over the past couple of weeks, and giving birth to Piper and Poppy was only the beginning of it. In addition to the physical toll of the experience, her emotions had ebbed and flowed like the tide. Except that suggested a predictable and almost gentle rhythm, whereas her moods had been anything but. Perhaps a more appropriate analogy would be the heart-pounding climbs and breath-stealing plunges of a roller coaster—like Space Mountain, completely in the dark.

Not that any of that dampened his desire for her. He only had to look at her to want her again. In fact, his body was already stirring, urging him to stretch out beside her and pick up where they'd left off.

Instead, he picked up the blanket that was neatly folded at the foot of the bed and gently draped it over her sleeping form, accepting his own unfulfilled desire as the price he had to pay for the bargain he'd struck. Because he knew that getting tangled up in a physical relationship with his wife would only make it that much harder for both of them when she eventually decided that she wanted to extricate herself from their marriage.

Because he'd been convinced, when they exchanged their vows, that the arrangement was only a temporary one. Not that she'd suggested any particular time frame, but he felt certain the day would come when she no longer wanted to be tied down to a man who was so wholly unsuitable. When she was more comfortable with and confident in her role as a mother and accepted that the difficulties of raising twin daughters on her own was less of a trial than staying with a man she didn't love.

Maybe, lately, he'd started to let himself imagine that they could make their marriage work—and admit to himself that he wanted to. Since sharing his home with Regan—and now their babies—he'd realized how empty his life had been before, without her in it. But Regan had given him no indication that the vows they'd exchanged meant anything more to her than a means to an end.

As Connor made his way back down the stairs, leaving his exhausted wife sleeping, he silently cursed Ben Channing for forcing him into this impossible situation.

Except that no one had forced him to do anything, his conscience reminded him. He'd taken the easy way. He'd sold out.

His conscience was right.

He should have spoken up and corrected the assumption that he was the father of Regan's babies when she first told her parents about the pregnancy. He should have made the truth known, loudly and clearly, because even when he'd acceded to her wordless request, he'd suspected his silence in that moment was going to come back to bite him.

As he passed the laundry room, he noticed an empty basket beside the dryer—a telltale sign that there was a load in need of folding. Diaper shirts and sleepers, he guessed. Because there always seemed to be a load of diaper shirts and sleepers in the laundry.

He transferred the contents of the dryer to the basket and carried it into the living room. He found a baseball game on TV and listened to the play-by-play as he folded the tiny garments—and a couple of even tinier pairs of bikini panties that obviously belonged to his wife.

He didn't know how to fold women's underwear—or even if they should be folded—so he simply made a neat pile of the panties and tried not to notice the silkiness of the fabric and peekaboo lace details. Because being in a marriage of convenience with a woman he wanted more than any other was painful enough without thinking about the sexy garments that hugged her feminine curves.

The fact that she wanted him, too—as she'd made abundantly clear before Baxter's interruption—only made their situation more difficult. While the sharing of physical intimacy would satisfy certain needs, Connor knew that the secret he continued to keep prevented them from developing a real and honest relationship.

A secret that dated back to the day after Regan's ultrasound, when Connor looked up from the report he was writing to see her father striding toward his desk. He'd been pretty sure he could guess why the man was there—but at least he wasn't carrying a shotgun.

The sheriff had offered his office for a more private conversation, and Connor had braced himself as he closed the door.

Regan's father had surprised him then by asking how

his brother was doing at Columbia and commiserating with the deputy about the outrageous costs of a college education—especially a top-notch law school like Columbia. And just when he'd started to think that he might have been mistaken about the reason for this visit, the other man asked if Deacon knew that Connor had put a second mortgage on his house to pay his brother's tuition.

Connor had admitted that he didn't and that he'd prefer to keep it that way. He hadn't bothered to ask how Regan's father knew about his financial situation. Ben Channing was a major shareholder in the local bank and his signature was required for most mortgages and loans.

The other man had acknowledged his request with a nod before unnecessarily pointing out that there wasn't enough equity in the property to finance a second year at Columbia.

And then he'd spoken the words that changed everything.

"Blake Mining is always looking for ways to give back to the community," Ben said. "And I'm confident that a scholarship fund to help with your brother's education would be a good use of our resources."

Connor had been intrigued by the idea—and more than a little wary. "Do you really think your company would be willing to give Deacon a scholarship?"

"If you help me, I'll help him."

Said the spider to the fly, Connor mused.

But still, he had to know: "What is it you think I can do for you?"

"Marry my daughter," Ben said.

Connor had, of course, anticipated this demand. And if the man had shown up with a shotgun in hand, he would have refused, for a lot of valid reasons. Instead,

Regan's father had come armed with something much more dangerous.

"How do you think your daughter would feel if she knew you were here trying to buy her a husband?" Connor had asked him.

"I don't imagine she'd be too happy," Ben admitted. "Which is why I'd appreciate your discretion."

"The situation isn't as black-and-white as you seem to think," he cautioned.

"I'm aware of the many shades of gray," the other man assured him. "And I'm not nearly as oblivious to what goes on in my daughter's life as she thinks. Thankfully, no one else knows about the short-term romantic relationship she ended a few months back.

"So when news of her pregnancy spreads, there's going to be talk and speculation about the father. If you put a ring on her finger, people will assume that the two of you did a remarkable job of keeping your relationship discreet."

"Why me?" Connor asked.

"Aside from what I said earlier about each of us being able to help the other, it occurred to me that you must care about Regan if you were willing to let her drag you into our home to announce her pregnancy, and then not correct our mistaken assumption that you were responsible."

"I didn't want to be there," Connor admitted. "But your daughter can be rather persuasive."

"Now it's your turn to persuade her that marrying you would be the best thing for her unborn children."

"How am I supposed to do that?"

"I don't think it will be too difficult," Ben said. "For all her courage and conviction, Regan's very much a traditional girl at heart. Given the choice, she'll want her babies to have both a mother and a father. A family."

Then he reached into his pocket and pulled out a check in an amount that made Connor's brows lift.

"I'm on my way to the bank now, to give the manager this. It only represents about half the costs of your brother's first year of law school," Ben acknowledged. "Consider it a sign of good faith. As soon as Regan's wearing your ring on her finger, your brother will get the other half. Just remember—she can't know that we had this conversation."

"You want me to lie to my prospective bride—your daughter—about my reasons for proposing to her? *If* I decide to go along with this plan," he hastened to clarify.

"I want you to make a case in favor of a legal union that will give her and her babies the security of a family and that will give you legitimacy in the eyes of the community."

And there it was—the acknowledgment that no matter how hard Connor had worked to turn his life around, to most of the residents of Haven, he was still just Faithless Faith's bastard son.

"I'm surprised you'd want your daughter to marry a man of questionable reputation," he'd remarked.

"I put more stock in character than reputation," Ben told him.

"A man of strong character wouldn't let himself be bought," Connor noted.

And before Ben Channing had pulled out that check, he would have said that he wasn't for sale. He was ashamed to acknowledge now that his assertion would have been wrong.

"Every man can be bought for the right currency."

For Connor, that currency had been his brother's education. Because Ben Channing was right—he'd had no idea how he would manage to pay for Deacon's second year of law school when he'd barely been scraping by after helping to finance his first semester.

And maybe, selfishly, he did crave the legitimacy that he knew marriage to Regan would bring.

So he'd taken the last of his meager savings and bought a ring.

He'd sold out.

He'd convinced himself that he was doing Regan a favor. That he was being noble and self-sacrificing. But the truth was, his actions had been selfish and self-serving. And yet, he'd been rewarded with a beautiful wife and two adorable babies.

He'd been fascinated by the twins since that very first ultrasound, and he'd become more and more enchanted as their growth and development was reflected in the changes to Regan's body. And when Piper and Poppy were finally born, the rush of emotion filled his heart to overflowing. He truly did love those baby girls as if they were his own. And watching his wife with their babies, he realized that he was developing some pretty deep feelings for Regan, too.

And that was before she'd kissed him tonight, tempting him with possibilities that he hadn't let himself even dream about.

There were days when he wondered how he'd let himself get caught up in the drama of her life and what his life would be like if he'd never made the trip to Battle Mountain for her ultrasound. But he couldn't imagine not having been there every day over the past several months.

And maybe that had been his punishment: being married to a warm, sexy woman that he couldn't touch.

Until today, when she'd suddenly changed all the rules.

When she'd turned his whole world upside down with a kiss.

Just thinking about those soft, sweet lips against his was enough to have the blood in his head migrating south. He didn't dare remember the press of her body against his, the glorious weight of those plump breasts filling his palms, the tantalizing rhythm of her pelvis rocking against his. The not remembering required so much effort that perspiration beaded on his brow.

As she'd pointed out to him earlier, there were different ways to finish, and he was going to have to utilize the old standby of teenage boys if he hoped to get any sleep tonight. But there would be no pretending that his callused hand could replicate her soft, tempting touch.

And that was probably for the best.

By her own admission, Regan had been feeling a little out of sorts after the family gathering at her parents' house. Maybe she wanted to pretend—at least for a while—that she had a real marriage like each of her brothers with their respective wives. The important thing for Connor to remember was that whatever she was feeling, it wasn't about him.

It had never been about him.

Theirs was just a marriage of convenience that was becoming more and more inconvenient with every day that passed.

Chapter Ten

Connor was up early after a restless night. As he moved down the hall past the master bedroom, he heard no sound from inside, suggesting that Regan and the twins were still asleep. He'd heard the babies in the wee hours and had felt a little guilty for leaving Regan to respond to their demands on her own. But apparently his self-preservation instincts were stronger than his sense of responsibility, because he hadn't gotten up to help. Because he didn't trust himself to walk away from her again if she invited him to share her bed.

He poured water into the coffeemaker, measured the grounds into the filter, then retrieved Baxter's leash from the hook by the door. The dog trotted happily along with his tongue hanging out of his mouth and his tail wagging.

As they made their way down Elderberry Lane, Connor noted an unfamiliar red Toyota pull into Bruce Ackerman's driveway. A slender woman with long blond hair got out of the driver's side and moved around to the back of the vehicle.

As she lifted a bucket of cleaning supplies out of the trunk, Connor thought there was something familiar about her. A gust of wind swept through the air, and she lifted a hand to tuck an errant strand of hair behind her ear.

The movement afforded him a clearer view of her profile and revealed why she seemed familiar. Mallory

Stillwell had lived across the street and two doors down from Connor while they were growing up. Though she was two years younger than he, they'd frequently hung out together and even dated for a brief while.

He'd lost touch with her after high school. The last he'd heard, she'd taken off for Vegas in the hopes of making a fortune—or at least a better life for herself. He didn't know if she'd found what she was looking for, but she was obviously back in Haven now.

"Mallory." He called out her name as he made his way down the street.

She didn't hear him.

Or maybe she was ignoring him, because she slammed the lid of the trunk and hurried toward the front of the house with the bucket in hand.

"Mallory," he called again, jogging to catch up with her.

Baxter barked happily, always eager to run.

She'd ignored Connor—twice, but the bark seemed to give her pause, reminding him that she'd always had a soft spot for animals.

In fact, she'd volunteered at the local animal shelter twice a week throughout high school. Of course, she'd said that anything was better than hanging around at home, deliberately downplaying the value of her efforts. He'd stopped by the shelter a couple of times to see her and noticed that she had tremendous empathy for all the animals, especially those that exhibited obvious signs of abuse.

She wasn't looking at him now, but at his canine companion. "Rusty?" she said, her voice hesitant.

Baxter barked and wagged his tail.

"Ohmygod…it *is* you." She dropped to her knees on

the driveway to embrace him, tears sliding down her cheeks.

"How do you know my dog?" Connor asked cautiously.

She wiped the backs of her hands over her tear-streaked cheeks before finally looking up at him. "He used to be my dog," she admitted. "Where did you find him? *When* did you find him?"

"Last April," he said. "Out at the train yard."

"Oh, Rusty," she said, her eyes filling with fresh tears.

"His name's Baxter now," Connor told her.

"Baxter," she echoed, and nodded. "It's a good name. He's a good dog."

"The best," Connor said. "So…how did he end up at the train yard?"

Her gaze skittered away. "I don't know."

"But you have a theory," he guessed.

"Evan said he ran away." She shrugged her narrow shoulders. "I suspected he left the door open on purpose, so that Rusty could do just that."

"Evan?" he prompted.

"My husband."

He glanced at her left hand, noted there was a thin gold band encircling her third finger.

"He was tied to a fence post," Connor told her. "Shivering. Starving."

She flinched, as if each word was a physical blow. "Evan never wanted a dog," she admitted, stroking her hands over Baxter's glossy coat as she spoke. "I picked Rusty—*Baxter*," she immediately corrected herself, "out of a litter of puppies that I helped take care of at the SPCA in Vegas, where we were living at the time. Evan was driving a rig and sometimes gone for weeks at a time, and I thought a dog would be good company for me and my daughter."

"I didn't know you had a child," he admitted.

Mallory nodded, her expression brightening slightly. "Chloe's almost six and the light of my life. When Rus—*Baxter* went missing, we were out all night looking for him. And again the next day, and the day after that."

She tipped her head forward, so that her face was curtained by her hair. "I thought Evan—" her voice broke and she shook her head, as if unable to complete the thought. "I'm so glad he's got a good home now." She looked up at him then and managed a tentative smile. "Good people."

"He does," Connor agreed. Then, "So what brought you back to Haven?"

"My mom died and left the house to me and my sisters, but they have better places to live. Madison's in Houston and Miranda's in Battle Mountain, so now I'm paying them rent to live in a house I didn't ever want to come back to." This time her shrug was one of resignation. "But Evan didn't grow up in Haven, and he figured that if we missed one or two rent payments here, my sisters wouldn't evict us."

"Is he still driving a rig?"

She shook her head. "His CDL was yanked for DUI. He's applied for a few jobs around town, but there aren't many."

They both knew the town's biggest employer was Blake Mining and that his wife was a Blake, so Connor had to give her credit for not attempting to leverage their shared history into a job for her husband.

"You've done good for yourself, though," Mallory noted, in an obvious effort to shift the conversation. "Working in the sheriff's office now, living in a house on the right side of town, married with children. Of course, no one was more surprised than me to hear that the Channing ice princess went slumming and got herself knocked up by my first boyfriend."

"Regan's a good person," he told her. "And a wonderful mother."

"Maybe, but those names—" she rolled her eyes "—Piper and Poppy? What were you thinking?"

"Piper's full name is Piper Faith Neal."

"Oh." Her sneer immediately faded. "For your mom. That's nice."

"It was Regan's idea."

"So maybe she's not all bad," Mallory allowed.

"She's amazing," Connor said.

She tilted her head to look at him. "Huh."

"What's that supposed to mean?"

"I guess I just assumed that you'd married her because she was pregnant. I never considered that you might actually have feelings for her."

Before he could respond to that, the front door opened and Mr. Ackerman poked his head out. "Everything okay, Mallory?"

"Just catching up with an old friend," she told him.

"I'm not paying you to chitchat, you know."

"I also know that you pay me by the job not the hour," she retorted. "So it doesn't really matter when I get started as long as the job gets done."

"Cheeky girl," the old man grumbled, with a twinkle in his eye.

"But I probably should get started," Mallory said, when Mr. Ackerman had disappeared back inside. "This is only the first of three houses I have to do today."

Connor nodded. "It was good to see you, Mallory."

"You, too." She looked at the dog at his feet and gave his head a quick rub. "And especially you, Baxter."

As Connor headed toward home, Mallory's comment about his feelings for Regan continued to echo in the back of his mind.

Of course he had feelings for Regan—but he wasn't inclined to put a label on those feelings.

He cared about her and enjoyed spending time with her. And why wouldn't he? She was beautiful and smart, with a generally sunny disposition and good sense of humor. She was also sexy as hell, and his attraction to her often felt like more of a curse than a blessing.

But for the better part of seven months, he'd managed to ignore the attraction. He'd ruthlessly shoved it aside, reminding himself that she'd married him not because she wanted a husband but because she wanted a father for her babies.

Their hasty vows had offered her a degree of protection when she could no longer hide her pregnancy. Sure, there was plenty of gossip as residents pretended to be shocked when they counted the months between the wedding and the birth of her babies and came up with a number less than nine. But the revelation that Regan Channing *had to* marry Connor Neal was scandalous enough that they didn't suspect there was more to the story.

Connor knew the whole truth, and that was a burden he carried alone. Regan had shared her deepest secrets with him, trusting that he would keep them safe. But he couldn't do the same, because his secrets—if revealed— could tear apart the fragile foundation of their family.

Maybe that foundation would be stronger if he'd been honest with her from the beginning. Instead, they'd built their marriage on secrets and lies. It was ironic, because he'd urged her to tell the truth to her parents, and when she'd stopped by to tell him that she was going to do just that, he was the one who backtracked from his own advice.

Twenty-four hours after Ben Channing's visit to the sheriff's office, Connor had been mulling over the man's proposition when Regan showed up at his door.

She'd offered him two containers of ice cream and a tempting smile. "Rocky road and chocolate."

"What's the occasion?" he'd asked.

"I've decided to tell my parents the truth tonight," she told him.

Baxter had been out in the backyard taking care of business, but he came through the doggy door then, and sensing—or maybe scenting—they had a visitor, raced to the front entrance as Regan stepped inside.

Before Connor could caution her or restrain the dog, Regan had dropped to her knees to fuss over the excited canine.

"Oh, aren't you just the cutest thing?" she'd said, clearly talking to the dog and not him. "And friendly," she noted with a chuckle, as she rubbed the back of her hand over her cheek to wipe away his slobbery doggy kisses.

"Baxter, sit."

The dog plopped his butt on the floor, but his tail continued to wag.

"He's very well trained," she'd remarked, rising to her feet.

"If he was well trained, you wouldn't have dog hair all over you," he'd noted.

Regan had glanced down and, with a dismissive shrug, brushed her hands over the thighs of her pants.

It might have been that moment, Connor realized now, when he really started to fall for her. Because who wouldn't fall for a beautiful, sexy woman who showed up at his door with ice cream and didn't mind his canine companion shedding all over her clothes?

His own hands had started to go numb from the cold, reminding him of the ice cream he was holding.

"What kind do you want?" he'd asked, leading the way to the kitchen.

"Can I have a scoop of each?"

He took two bowls out of the cupboard. "I thought you weren't one of those women who drowns her worries with copious amounts of chocolate."

"If I wanted to do that, I would have stayed home with both containers and a spoon," she'd said.

He'd chuckled at her remark as he pried the lid off the first container and dipped the scoop inside.

"So why today?" he'd asked, when he handed her the bowl full of ice cream and a spoon.

"I figured, after three days, my father's blood pressure should have come down to something approximating normal. And I know you're anxious for me to rectify their misunderstanding."

Of course, he'd urged her to do exactly that—but that was before Ben Channing had shown up at the sheriff's office with his intriguing proposition.

"So tell me," she said, apparently wanting to discuss something other than the impending visit with her parents. "Was this circa 1980 kitchen a deliberate design choice?"

"Actually, I think it's circa 1972, because that's when the house was built."

She glanced around. "You're not interested in updating the look?"

"It's functional," he said, well aware that the space was in desperate need of a major overhaul. But right now,

Connor could hardly afford a can of paint, never mind a more substantial renovation.

Except that Deacon had called him that afternoon, practically bursting with excitement over the news that he'd been awarded another scholarship—confirming that Ben Channing had honored at least the first part of his promise. Deacon wanted to send the money back to his brother, to repay him for his first-term tuition. But Connor had suggested that he hold on to the funds for second term, because he knew it might be the last "Aim Higher" check he ever saw.

Of course, that scholarship depended on Connor more than Deacon. All he had to do was convince Regan to marry him, and her father would ensure that Blake Mining continued to fund the scholarship.

Sure, he had qualms about proposing for mercenary reasons. Truthfully, he had qualms about marriage in general. And a lot of reservations about his ability to fulfill the responsibilities of parenthood. Because what did he know about being a father? His biological father had never been part of his life and his stepfather had been an abusive drunk, ensuring he had no role models he'd want to emulate.

But something had happened when he'd seen Regan's babies on the ultrasound monitor. He'd felt an unexpected swell of emotion, a desire to help and protect both the mom and her babies. Maybe he didn't know anything about being a dad, but he knew that if he was ever entrusted with the care of a child—or children, he would do everything in his power to be the best dad that he could be.

"Did you stop by to critique my decor?" he'd asked Regan, picking up the thread of their conversation.

"No." She'd sighed. "My visit was solely for the purposes of procrastination—and ice cream."

"You're not eager to tell your parents the truth," he'd guessed.

"Definitely not," she agreed. "When my dad hears that you're not the father of my baby, he's going to demand to know who is, so that he can force me to marry him."

"You don't want to marry the father?"

"Not an option," she said bluntly.

"Why not?" he wondered.

"Because bigamy's illegal in Nevada."

And he'd thought nothing could have surprised him more than her pregnancy. "He's married?"

She'd nodded slowly. "I didn't know he was married when we were together," she explained. "But maybe I should have suspected something was up.

"He was an environmental consultant in town on a contractual assignment, and because he was only going to be in town for a short while, he wanted to be discreet. To protect my reputation, he said, because he understood how gossip worked in small towns and he didn't want people talking about me.

"In retrospect, it was obvious that he didn't want people talking about *us*, because some people did know that he was married."

"When did you find out?" Connor asked her.

"When I told him that I was pregnant," she admitted. "Our relationship was already over, but when I realized I was going to have his baby, I went to see him."

She shoveled another spoonful of ice cream into her mouth. "I didn't want or expect anything from him—not that I was willing to admit, anyway—but I felt I had an obligation to tell him that he was going to be a father." She swirled her spoon inside the bowl. "Turned out he didn't just have a wife but two kids—and he didn't want any more. And he definitely didn't want me causing any trouble for his perfect little family.

"He used me," she said quietly. "And I was foolish enough to let him."

He'd never seen her like this—so vulnerable and insecure. Even when she'd been throwing up outside of Diggers', she'd given the impression of a woman in control of her life—if not her morning sickness. Even at the clinic for her ultrasound, she'd seemed appreciative of his support but not in need of it. And her sudden openness and uncertainty now brought out every protective instinct he had, urging him to help her in any way that he could.

She dropped her gaze to the remnants of the ice cream, then pushed the bowl away, her craving sated—or maybe her appetite lost.

"I just wish there was a way to be sure he couldn't ever make a claim to my babies."

"Do you have any reason to suspect that he would?"

"No," she admitted. "He was pretty adamant that he wanted nothing to do with another child. I just hate to imagine what might happen if he ever changed his mind."

And Connor hated that she'd just given him leverage to push his own agenda, but that didn't prevent him from using it. "I'm not a lawyer, but I know there's something called a presumption of paternity," he'd told her. "If a man is married to a woman when she gives birth, he is presumed, in the eyes of the law, to be the father. If you want to be sure this guy can't make a claim to your babies, you could marry someone else before they're born and put your husband's name on their birth certificates."

Regan had seemed intrigued by the idea at first, but after another moment of consideration, she'd shaken her head. "I don't think I could trick some hapless guy into marrying me."

"You don't have to trick anyone," Connor had assured her then. "You could marry *me*."

Chapter Eleven

"I was starting to worry that you might have gotten lost," Regan said to Connor, when he returned from his walk the next morning.

Baxter raced over to her chair for the pat on the head that he figured was his due. Then he raced into the living room, no doubt looking for the twins, and upstairs to the master bedroom, where he dropped to the floor to stand guard in his usual position outside the door after finding them.

Connor washed his hands at the sink, then retrieved a mug from the cupboard and filled it with coffee. "I ran into an old friend from high school."

She didn't ask if it was anyone she knew, because there had been little—if any—overlap between their social circles when they were teenagers.

"Do you want me to make you some breakfast?" she asked.

"Mmm…" He sounded intrigued by the offer. "Belgian waffles with fresh berries and powdered sugar would be good."

"You had Belgian waffles at brunch yesterday," she reminded him. "How about scrambled eggs and toast?"

"Eggs and toast sound good, too," he agreed. "But I'll make them."

"I know how to break eggs," she remarked dryly.

"You're also going to be up and down with the twins

all day, so why don't you sit for ten minutes and let me take care of breakfast?"

It sounded perfectly reasonable—considerate, even. And yet, she couldn't help but wonder if this was another example of her husband attempting to ensure that they didn't fall into any kind of usual married couple routines.

"I'm not fragile, Connor."

"I know."

"And I don't need you to take care of me."

"Maybe I want to," he said. "It seems only fair, since you spend so much time taking care of Piper and Poppy."

She shrugged. "In that case, I like my eggs with Tabasco mixed in and cheese melted on top."

He set a frying pan on the stove to heat, then retrieved the necessary ingredients from the fridge.

"I'm sorry about last night," she said, as he whisked the eggs. "Not about what happened—or almost happened—but about the interruption."

"There's no need to apologize." He shook a few drops of Tabasco into the egg mixture and continued whisking. "And anyway, it was probably best that we didn't take things too far."

She frowned at that. "How's that best?"

"Getting intimate would only complicate our situation," he explained, as he dropped bread into the slots of the toaster.

"We're married. Isn't physical intimacy usually a key component of that situation?"

"Except that ours isn't a usual marriage," he reminded her.

"I'll concede that sex usually comes before marriage and children," she said.

He poured the egg mixture into the hot pan. "And you only gave birth two weeks ago," he reminded her.

"What does that have to do with anything?"

"Pregnancy and childbirth take a toll on your body, not just physically but emotionally, and it's going to take some time for your hormone levels to recalibrate and—"

"You're not seriously trying to explain postpartum physiology to me, are you?" she asked, cutting him off.

"Of course not," he denied, as he pushed the eggs around in the pan with the spatula. "I just want you to know that I understand what happened last night wasn't really about us as much as it was a reaction to the emotional stresses of the day."

"Have you been reading my pregnancy and childcare books again?"

"I thought you wanted me to read them."

"To learn about the growth and development of the babies—not about what exercises help strengthen pelvic floor muscles or how long it takes for a uterus to shrink back to its normal size," she told him.

"Kegels, and about a month," he said, as he grated cheese over the eggs.

She huffed out a breath. "Okay, you get a gold star for that. But the implication that what happened last night was about nothing more than hormones is insulting to both of us.

"Maybe I was an idiot for wanting to feel close to my husband," she continued. "But you don't need to worry— it's not likely a mistake I'll make again."

She pushed back her chair as the toast popped up.

Connor transferred the eggs to a plate. "Your breakfast is ready," he said.

"I'm not hungry," she snapped, as she moved past him toward the stairs.

Which, of course, only proved that he was right.

* * *

Regan was just sliding Estela Lopez's chicken pot pie into the oven when her husband got home from work. She'd moved the babies' bassinet into the kitchen so that she could keep an eye on them while she peeled potatoes—which meant that Baxter was close by, too.

Connor offered her a smile when he entered the kitchen, then set a cylindrical tube on the table as he bent to give Baxter a scratch.

He'd made the first overture, and she knew that the next step needed to be hers.

"I'm sorry," she said.

He rose to his full height again and turned to face her, tucking his hands into his front pockets. "Isn't this how our conversation started this morning?" he asked warily.

She poked at the potatoes with a fork, checking them for doneness. "That's why I'm apologizing."

"Should I tell you again that it's not necessary?"

"But it is," she insisted, setting the fork down again and moving away from the heat of the stove. "Once I had some time to calm down and think about what you were saying, I realized that you were trying to be considerate of my feelings—physically and emotionally."

He nodded slowly.

"So I apologize for overreacting and storming out of the room," she said. And though she knew she should leave it at that, she couldn't resist adding, "But I'm still annoyed that you didn't give me credit for knowing my own feelings."

"Then I will apologize for that," he told her. "And, since we're clearing the air…"

She looked up, waiting for him to continue.

But instead of saying anything else, he pulled her close and kissed her.

It happened so fast—or maybe the move was just so completely unexpected—that she wasn't sure how to respond.

The touch of his mouth, warm and firm, wiped all thought from her mind. Desire tightened in her belly, then slowly unfurled like a ribbon, spreading from her center to the tips of her fingers and toes and every part in between. Just as she started to melt against him, he lifted his mouth from hers and took a deliberate step back.

She caught her bottom lip, still tingling from his kiss, in her teeth and lifted her gaze to his.

"What—" She cleared her throat. "What was that about?"

"I didn't want there to be any doubt about my attraction to you."

"Point taken," she told him.

He nodded. "Good. Also—" he picked up the tube again "—I have a peace offering."

"It doesn't look like flowers or jewelry," she noted, trying to match his casual tone though her insides were all tangled up from his kiss.

"I think it's something you'll like much better."

"Now my curiosity is definitely piqued."

He lifted the cap off the tube and pulled out—

"The blueprints for the kitchen?" she guessed.

He nodded.

He'd shown her the plans a few months earlier, when she'd lamented the sorry state of the kitchen cabinets after one of the doors almost came off its hinges in her hand. Apparently he did aspire to a cooking and eating space that was more than functional, but the price tag of a major renovation had forced him to delay implementing his plans.

"But...you said you couldn't afford to make any big

changes right now," she said, hating to remind him of the fact.

"Because I couldn't, but Deacon paid me back for his tuition when his scholarship came through, and now I can."

"I'd say that scholarship was a stroke of luck, but I have no doubt Deacon earned it through hard work rather than good fortune."

Connor busied himself unrolling the papers. "He's always been a good student—diligent and conscientious."

"And it paid off," she said.

"So it would seem," he agreed.

"I know I've said it before, but I'd be happy to—"

"No," he interrupted.

"But I could easily—"

"No," he cut her off again.

Regan huffed out a breath. "Why are you being so bullheaded about this?"

"Because I don't want you to think that I married you for your money."

"The prenup you insisted on made that perfectly clear."

"Good." He nodded again, indicating that the subject was closed. "But there is one other thing we need to discuss."

"What's that?" She dumped the potatoes into a colander to drain the water, then returned them to the pot and added butter and milk.

"If we're going to move ahead with the renovations, you can't stay here," he told her.

She frowned as he retrieved the masher from the utensil holder and took the pot from her to finish the potatoes.

"Why not?"

"Because it's not healthy for you and the babies to be living in a construction zone."

"Where are we supposed to go?" she asked.

"The easiest solution would probably be Miners' Pass." He added salt and pepper to the pot.

"You want me to take Piper and Poppy and move back to my parents' place?"

"Only temporarily," he said.

"Now I have to wonder if your impulsive decision to renovate is about updating the kitchen or putting some distance between us."

"Maybe both," he acknowledged.

"Well, at least you're honest."

Maybe he was right. Maybe the forced proximity during Brielle's visit had stirred up something that would have been better left alone. And maybe a couple of weeks apart would be good for them—with the added benefit that she would come home to a new kitchen.

"So which plan are you going with?" she asked. "The one with the walk-in pantry or the one with the island?"

"Which one do you want?"

"You're letting me choose?"

"It's your kitchen, too," he reminded her.

"I want the island," she immediately responded. Then reconsidered. "But the walk-in pantry is a really nice feature, too."

"I thought you'd say that." He gestured to the blueprints, encouraging her to look at them again.

It was then that she noticed there were now *three* sets of plans.

"I asked Kevin to come up with a new design that incorporated all of the elements you seemed to like best from the first two plans."

She moved for a closer look. "Oh, Connor…this is perfect!"

"And now you know my decision to renovate wasn't

as impulsive as you think. In fact, the cabinets should be ready next week, which means these ones need to be ripped out this weekend so the tile people can come on Monday."

She threw her arms around him. "Okay. I'll take the babies to my parents' house," she agreed, because she definitely didn't want their newborn lungs breathing in construction dust and paint fumes. "But I want to help. What can I do?"

"You can pick out the paint."

She was tempted to roll her eyes but managed to restrain herself, because she did like the idea of choosing the color for the walls. And they'd need a new covering for the window—maybe a California-style shutter to replace the roll-up bamboo shade that she suspected had been put in place by the original owners.

The plans called for slate-colored floor tiles, glossy white cabinets with stainless-steel handles and countertops of dark gray granite with blue flecks. She could already picture the finished room with cobalt blue and sunny yellow accents.

"And maybe I can get new dishes for the new kitchen," she said.

"What's wrong with my dishes?"

"Aside from the fact that they're *your* dishes, I don't think there are any two plates or bowls that match."

"Who cares if they match?" He immediately read her response to that question in her expression. "Okay, if you want new dishes for your new kitchen, you can buy new dishes."

"And glasses and cutlery?"

"And glasses and cutlery," he confirmed.

She narrowed her gaze. "Why are you suddenly letting me do this?"

"Because you're right—everything in this kitchen, in this house, was here before you moved in, when it was *my* house. Now it's *our* house, and I want you to do whatever you need to do to feel as if it's your home, too."

"That makes me feel a little bit better about the fact that you're kicking me out of *our* house for the next couple of weeks," she said.

"You wanted the new kitchen," he reminded her.

"Then I guess the lesson to be learned from this is that I shouldn't give up hope of getting what I want." She leaned across the counter and brushed her lips over his. "A lesson I will definitely keep in mind."

With a light step and smug smile, she moved away to take the casserole out of the oven, making Connor suspect that she wasn't only thinking about the kitchen renovation.

It felt strange to be back in her parents' house again.

Though she'd lived there for three years prior to marrying Connor and moving in with him, the mansion had never felt like home. It was an impressive structure built with meticulous attention by reputable craftsmen, the interior professionally finished and elaborately decorated with no expense spared. The result was a stunning presentation suitable to a spread in *Architectural Digest* but lacking any sense of history or feeling of warmth.

She'd set up the portable playpen in the great room, close enough to the fire to ensure the babies wouldn't catch a chill, while she brought in the rest of their things. The housekeeper had helped unload the cases from her trunk and promised to move them upstairs as soon as she had Regan's bed made up. Ordinarily Regan would have insisted on carrying them herself, but as the babies were starting to fuss for their dinner, she was grateful for Greta's help.

She'd finished nursing and had settled them down again when she heard the door from the garage open and the voices of her parents as they came in. From the sound of it, she was the topic of their conversation.

"—she was coming?" Ben asked.

"No," his wife replied. "If I'd known she was coming, I would have told you."

"Maybe it's not her car."

Margaret huffed out a breath. "Of course it's her car."

"Hi, Mom. Hi, Dad," she called out.

Her mother's heels clicked on the marble tile as she drew nearer.

Margaret stopped abruptly and pivoted to look at her husband. "I told you this would happen."

"Let's not jump to conclusions," Ben cautioned.

"What do you think happened?" Regan asked curiously.

Her mother waved a hand at the pile of bags and baby paraphernalia beside the door—the size of which had already been reduced by half by the diligent efforts of the housekeeper.

"Obviously you've left your husband. Not that I'm surprised, really, except maybe by the fact that the marriage lasted a whole six months."

"Please, Mom. Don't hold back—tell me what you really think."

"I'm sorry," Margaret said, not sounding sorry at all. "But if you'd bothered to talk to me before running off and getting married, I would have told you that you were making a mistake and you wouldn't be in this mess right now."

"I didn't leave my husband, and I'm not in a mess,"

Regan told her, speaking slowly and carefully so as not to reveal the hurt and disappointment elicited by her mother's assumptions. "The only mess is going to be in our kitchen, while Connor oversees the renovations. He suggested that I bring Piper and Poppy here for a couple of weeks so that we're not living in a construction zone."

There was a moment of stilted silence as her parents digested the information.

"Well, what was I supposed to think?" Margaret demanded without apology.

"I don't know," Regan admitted. "But I didn't expect you would immediately jump to the conclusion that my marriage had fallen apart."

"You might have called first to let someone know your plans," Ben suggested, his effort to smooth over the tension clearly placing the blame at Regan's feet.

"I did," she said. "I talked to Celeste."

"Has Greta made up your room?" Margaret asked.

"She said that she would," Regan replied. "But I can probably stay at Crooked Creek with Spencer and Kenzie, if you'd prefer."

"Don't be silly," her mother chided. "You don't want to be out in the middle of nowhere. Not to mention that we've got a lot more room for you and the twins here."

Regan nodded, because the latter statement at least was true. As for being out in the middle of nowhere— right now she wanted to be anywhere but here, but she wasn't foolish enough to bundle up her babies and pack up all their stuff again just because her feelings were hurt.

"I'll let Celeste know she can put dinner on the table," Margaret said now.

"She didn't mean anything by it," Ben said, when his wife had gone.

Regan just shook her head. "I don't understand. I thought you were happy that I married Connor."

"Under the circumstances, it seemed the best course of action," he said.

The circumstances being that she was pregnant, and they'd assumed—because she'd let them—that Connor was the father of her babies.

"He's a good man," Regan said now. "And I wouldn't have married him if I didn't believe we could make our marriage work."

He nodded. "I'm glad to hear it."

"And he's a wonderful father."

"Anyone who's ever seen him with your babies would agree with that," Ben assured her.

It was only later, when she was alone upstairs in her bed, that she wondered about his reference to Piper and Poppy as "her" babies.

Was it possible that her father knew more about her relationship with Connor than she'd told him?

"Damn, the house is quiet."

Connor didn't realize he'd spoken aloud until Baxter lifted his head off his paws and whined in agreement. He didn't believe the dog actually understood what he was saying, but he suspected his canine companion was responding to the regret in his tone.

"Maybe I didn't think this through enough," he acknowledged with a sigh. "I wanted to get the kitchen done because it seemed to mean a lot to Regan, but I also figured it would be easier to keep my hands off her if she was out of the house." He shook his head. "I just didn't expect it to feel so empty without her."

Baxter belly-shuffled closer, so that he was at his master's feet. Connor reached down and patted the dog's head.

Baxter immediately rolled over, exposing his belly for a rub.

Connor laughed and obliged. "Just like old times, huh? Just you and me?"

The dog whined again.

"It wasn't so bad back then, was it? At least we got to sleep through the night without being awakened by babies wanting to be fed or changed."

The dog looked at him with soulful eyes, clearly unconvinced.

"Okay, yeah. Maybe it didn't seem so bad back then because we didn't know anything different."

Baxter lowered his chin onto the top of Connor's foot.

"I'll get to work on the kitchen first thing in the morning," he promised. "Because the sooner I get started, the sooner I can finish, and Regan and Piper and Poppy can come home."

Chapter Twelve

Connor had just poured his first cup of coffee—not decaf but the real stuff, which he'd snuck into the house after a string of sleep-deprived nights made it almost impossible to keep his eyes open during the day—when there was a knock at the door.

"We've got an early-morning visitor," he said to Baxter, who was already jumping up at the front door.

"None of that," he said, giving the hand signal for sit.

The dog sat, though his body fairly vibrated with suppressed energy.

Connor unlocked and pulled open the door, surprised to see his boss on the other side of the threshold. "Good morning, Sheriff."

"Reid," he said, confirming that he wasn't at the door for any kind of official business. "I heard you talking to Kowalski about a demolition project you're tackling this weekend and thought maybe you could use a hand."

"Your wife doesn't have a list of chores for you at home?" Connor asked, opening the door wider to let him in.

"There's always a list," Reid said, and grinned at the dog sitting but not at all patiently inside the foyer.

He offered his hand for the dog to sniff, which Baxter did and gave his approval with a lick. The sheriff chuckled and scratched him under the chin.

"But Katelyn took Tessa out to the Circle G for a visit,"

Reid explained. "So she's not home today to remind me about all the things on the list."

Connor led the way to the kitchen. "So you came here to help with my list instead?"

"Tearing things apart is always more fun than putting them back together," Reid noted. "Although I have to say, it seems like an odd time to be tackling kitchen renovations—barely three weeks after the birth of twin daughters."

"Yeah," Connor agreed. He found another coffee mug in one of the boxes that he'd used to empty the cabinets and held it up, a silent question.

Reid nodded.

"But Regan would argue that updating the space is twenty years overdue," Connor continued, as he filled the second mug. "Notwithstanding the fact that I've only owned the house for three."

"Katelyn wouldn't move into our new place until all the work we wanted to do had been done. Thankfully, most of it was cosmetic."

"This is going to be a complete overhaul," Connor told him.

"You want to salvage the cabinets?" Reid asked.

He shook his head. "Not worth salvaging. Everything's going in the Dumpster."

"That will speed things up considerably," Reid said.

What also sped things up considerably was having an extra body pitching in. By the time they broke for lunch—Connor popped out to pick up Jo's Pizza—all of the top cabinets and half of the bottom had been removed and hauled out to the Dumpster.

As Connor closed the lid on the empty pizza box, the sheriff's phone chimed to indicate a message.

"Kate texted me a picture of Tessa with Ava, Max

and Sam," Reid said, turning his phone around so Connor could see the screen. "Tessa absolutely adores the triplets and is constantly asking to go see the babies. In fact, I think her favorite word now is *babies*. Although her first word was *Da-da*," he added, with a grin.

"Does it make you think about giving her a brother or sister?" Connor wondered.

"Sure," Reid agreed, as he tucked his phone away again. "But Katelyn's not yet on board with that plan. In all fairness, that might be because she tackles most of the childcare responsibilities. I've been encouraging her to check out the new daycare, but she insists that Tessa's too young to be left with strangers."

"A valid consideration," Connor noted, tugging his work gloves on again. "Though not a choice all parents can make."

Reid nodded. "But getting back to your question, yeah, I think Tessa would benefit from having a sibling."

"It is a unique bond," Connor noted. "Though I'll be the first to admit, I was a little panicked about the prospect of twins—"

"Especially twin girls, I'd bet," the sheriff interjected.

"You'd be right," Connor agreed. "But now I can appreciate how lucky Piper and Poppy are to have one another."

"They are lucky," Reid remarked. "I was an only child, so I didn't grow up with the benefit of knowing there was someone else who would always have my back. Of course, Katelyn had a sister and two brothers, so she wished sometimes that she was an only child."

Connor chuckled at that. "Well, there were eight years between me and Deacon, so that likely helped minimize any sibling rivalry."

"Speaking of—is your brother coming home for the summer?"

He nodded. "He was hoping to land a job in New York, something in the legal field for experience to add to his résumé, but nothing panned out."

"Katelyn's practice is growing like crazy, and she's been talking about wanting to hire a junior lawyer to help with research and case prep," Reid said. His wife was widely regarded as one of the top attorneys in the area and, as a result, her services were in great demand. "You should tell him to send his résumé to her."

"Deacon's hardly a junior lawyer," Connor pointed out. "He's only just finishing his first year of law school."

"First year at Columbia," his boss clarified. "That seems to me a pretty good recommendation right there."

"Well, he's obviously smarter than me, or I would have waited to tackle this renovation until he was home to help."

"On the other hand, there are certain therapeutic benefits of physical labor, which I'm sure you can appreciate right now."

Connor paused with the sledgehammer on his shoulder. "You're not really asking about my sex life, are you?"

"I don't need to ask," Reid told him. "I've been there. And I swear, those six weeks postpartum while we waited for the doctor to give us the green light were the longest six weeks of my life."

Six weeks?

Connor and Regan had been married for more than *six months* and hadn't even consummated their marriage—not that he had any intention of admitting that to his boss.

Instead, he responded by lifting the sledgehammer off his shoulder and heaving it at the wall marked to come down.

The plaster cracked and the sheriff laughed.

* * *

By her third day at Miners' Pass, most of the sting of her mother's words had faded, allowing Regan to acknowledge that it wasn't a horrible place to wait out the renovations. She didn't see much of her parents, who always went to the office early and came home late, but Celeste and Greta were more than happy to help with anything she needed or even just spend some time cuddling with the babies when they had nothing else to do.

But Monday was Celeste's grocery shopping day, so Regan had decided to go into town, too. She'd only been back a little while when Greta escorted a visitor to the great room, where Regan spent most of her time hanging out during the day.

"What are you doing here?" she asked, as pleased as she was surprised to see her husband.

"I came by to see if you've picked a paint color yet."

"As a matter of fact, I have." She reached into the side pocket of the diaper bag that was always close at hand and pulled out an assortment of paint chips. "I finally tried out that twin baby carrier we got from Alyssa and Jason, and Piper and Poppy had a great time being carted around the hardware store." She fanned out the samples, looking for the one she'd marked, then plucked it out of the pile and offered it to him. "Are you prepping to paint already?"

"Not even close," he admitted.

She lifted a brow. "So why are you really here?"

He shoved the paint chip in his back pocket without even looking at it. "Because I missed you."

"Oh." She felt an unexpected little flutter in her belly.

"Even with all the hammering and banging going on, I find myself listening for the familiar sounds of Piper and Poppy waking up or growing restless," he told her.

"You miss the babies," she realized, as the flutter faded away.

"I miss all of you," he clarified. "I miss the scent of your shampoo in the bathroom in the morning, the sound of your humming in the kitchen and the way your smile shines in your eyes."

And the flutter was back.

But still, she felt compelled to point out: "I don't hum."

He smiled. "Yeah, you do."

"And if you miss me, it's your own fault," she said. "Because you sent me away."

"I didn't know how empty the house was going to feel without you."

"You still have Baxter."

"He misses you as much as I do," he told her. "And a moping dog isn't very good company."

"You could bring him with you for a visit sometime," she said.

He looked pointedly at the cream-colored suede furniture on the ivory carpet and shook his head. "I don't think so."

"Then maybe I'll bring Piper and Poppy to your place—"

"*Our* place," he reminded her.

"—and take him out for a walk one day."

"He'd love that," Connor said. "But are you sure you can manage two babies and a dog?"

"With the twin carrier, I can," she assured him. "And speaking of the twins, I'm guessing you'd like to see them."

He grinned. "Well, I have no intention of leaving until I do."

She took his hand and led him upstairs. "Not because I want you to leave," she assured him. Piper and Poppy were sharing her former bedroom, where she'd taken up temporary residence again, and were snuggled together in the bassinet near the head of her bed. On the other side of the room was a rocking chair that Greta had brought up for the new mom.

Connor stood for a long moment, just looking at the sleeping babies. "I swear they've grown in the past three days." Though he whispered the remark, Piper stirred as if she'd heard and recognized her daddy's voice.

"Considering how often they're eating, I wouldn't be surprised," Regan told him. "But they're sleeping a little bit longer now. Last night it was almost five hours."

"Have they been asleep for long now?" he asked.

"I think what you really want to know is, are they going to be waking up soon?"

"Are they?"

She lifted a shoulder. "New moms who have their three-week-old babies on any kind of schedule are obviously better moms than me."

He shook his head. "There is no better mom than you."

"And that's why I'm going to risk breaking the rule about not disturbing a sleeping baby," she said, reaching down and gently lifting Piper out of the bassinet.

"But the books—"

"I'm going to hide those books from you," she said, gesturing toward the rocking chair.

He sat down and she transferred Piper to him, then went back to the bassinet for Poppy.

"They've had their baths already today," he noted.

"Maybe it's the scent of *their* shampoo that you remember," she teased.

"I can remember more than one scent," he told her. "Your shampoo smells like apples."

Poppy exhaled a quiet sigh and snuggled closer to her daddy's chest. Piper yawned.

"I think they missed you, too," Regan said quietly.

"I could sit here like this for hours," he said. "But that isn't going to get the new drywall taped and mudded."

"You're doing that yourself?"

He nodded. "It's not hard work, just messy, and it cuts down on the cost of labor."

"And you're going to tackle that tonight?"

"I'm going to get started anyway, as soon as I figure out what I'm doing for food."

"You could stay and have dinner with me," she suggested. "You know Celeste always makes enough for unexpected guests."

"I didn't come here to beg a meal," he assured her. "But it would be nice to eat something that wasn't Wheaties."

"Your dinner plan was Wheaties?"

"No, but I probably would have ended up eating Wheaties because I didn't have a dinner plan. And because I don't have a stove," he said, reminding her that the appliances had been taken out of the kitchen along with everything else.

"Then this is your lucky day," Regan said. "Because Celeste has a box of Frosted Flakes in the cupboard."

"Frosted Flakes are more a dessert than a main course."

"Beggars can't be choosers," she said.

Connor knew she was only teasing in quoting the old proverb, but there was something about being in this house that made him feel like a beggar—though he suspected a vagrant would never get past the housekeeper at the front door.

His mother, a big admirer of Eleanor Roosevelt, would

have pointed out that no one could make him feel unworthy without his consent. He knew it was true, that his insecurities said more about him than anyone else. And Regan had never said or done anything to indicate that she thought any less of him because he was "that no-good Neal boy" from "the wrong side of the tracks."

So he shook off the unease and carefully settled Piper and Poppy back in their bassinet, then followed his wife downstairs again and into the kitchen.

"Connor's going to stay for dinner," Regan said to the cook, who was drizzling caramel sauce over the top of a pie.

"And dessert," he added.

"You like pecan pie?" Celeste guessed.

"I like everything you make," he assured her.

She set the pie aside and reached into the cupboard for two plates. "It'll just take me a minute to set the table."

"The kitchen table is fine," Regan said, pulling open a drawer to retrieve cutlery.

"You know how your parents feel about eating in the kitchen," Celeste chided.

"I do, and since they're not going to be home for dinner, we'd like to eat in the kitchen—with you."

"You can eat wherever you like," the cook agreed. "But I'm having dinner in my room with *Top Chef.*"

"This is the first you've mentioned wanting to watch a cooking show tonight," Regan remarked.

"Because I didn't want you to have to eat your dinner alone. Since you now have the company of your handsome husband, you won't miss mine."

"Did you hear that?" Connor said to his wife. "She thinks I'm handsome."

"Just about handsome enough for my beautiful girl," Celeste confirmed.

"That's me," Regan told him.

The cook chuckled. "Now you two sit down and enjoy your dinner," she said, as she filled their plates with crispy honey garlic chicken, roasted potatoes and steamed broccoli.

Connor and Regan lingered over the meal, discussing all manner of topics.

"I'm doing all the talking," Connor realized, when his plate was half empty.

"Because your life is so much more interesting than mine right now," she told him. "You have an exciting job, a construction project underway and a faithful canine companion at home. My days are taken up by two admittedly adorable infants who eat, sleep, pee and poop—not necessarily in that order."

He chuckled, but then his expression turned serious. "Do you miss work?"

"Not yet," she said. "Right now I'm so tired out from keeping up with Piper and Poppy that the idea of going into the office and trying to make sense of numbers makes my head hurt."

She frowned as she lifted her glass of water to her lips. "But now that I think about it, there was a weird message on my voice mail the other day from one of the junior accountants at work. I haven't had a chance to call him back yet, but Travis's message said something about a scholarship fund."

The delicious chicken dinner suddenly felt like a lead weight in Connor's stomach. "He shouldn't be bothering you with trivial inquiries when you're on mat leave," he said. "Isn't there someone else who can answer his questions?"

"My father, probably," she said.

"Then you should let your father deal with it."

She nodded. "Yeah. When I get a chance to call Travis back, I'll tell him to talk to my dad."

"Or tell your dad about the call," he suggested. "And let him handle it."

"That's another option," she agreed.

He pushed his chair away from the table and stood up to clear away their plates.

"I suppose you want that pie now?" Regan asked.

"Actually, I didn't realize how late it was getting to be," he said. "If I want to make any progress with that drywall tonight, I should probably be heading out."

"You could take a slice with you," she offered. "We won't call it a doggy bag, so you won't feel obligated to share it with Baxter."

"I'd love to," he said. "It'll be my reward for getting the first layer of mud done."

She found a knife and cut a thick wedge of pie, which she slid into a plastic container. Just as she snapped the lid on, a soft, plaintive cry came through the baby monitor on the table.

"Well, we actually got through a meal without interruption," she said.

"It was a great meal," he said. "Thanks for asking me to stay."

"Thanks for stopping by." She started to walk with him to the door, but even he could tell that the cries were growing louder and more insistent. She folded an arm across her chest, her cheeks suddenly turning pink. "Letdown."

And because he'd read the books, he knew what that meant. "You better go see to the babies."

She nodded and turned to hurry up the stairs.

Connor was admittedly sorry that he hadn't had the chance to steal a goodbye kiss, but at the moment he had more pressing concerns. And a call to his father-in-law was at the top of the list.

When the two men had struck their deal, Connor hadn't given any thought to the possibility that Regan—Blake Mining's CFO—might question why a check written by her father from a company account had been deposited into an account with her husband's brother's name on it. So he hoped like hell Ben Channing had given the matter some thought—and had a credible explanation ready for his daughter if one was required.

Chapter Thirteen

Detouring to Miners' Pass became part of Connor's routine over the next couple of weeks. He never stayed long, as he was anxious to get back to work on the kitchen so that Regan and the twins could come home. But it was always worth the trip, just to spend a few minutes with them—with the added benefit of a fabulous meal that beat any kind of takeout.

He was usually gone before Regan's parents got home from the office. It seemed a shame to him that they'd spent so much money to build a beautiful home that was empty most of the time, but he got the impression that the display of wealth was almost more important to Margaret than the enjoyment of it.

In any event, he didn't mind not crossing paths with Ben and Margaret—no doubt at least in part because of his own guilt with respect to the secret he was keeping from his wife. No matter how many times Connor tried to reassure himself that the money Ben Channing had put up for Deacon's scholarship had nothing to do with his relationship with Regan, he knew it wasn't really true.

There would have been no scholarship if he hadn't convinced Regan to marry him, and lately, he'd found himself wishing that he'd never entered into any sort of agreement with his now father-in-law. He didn't regret his marriage to Regan. He just wished the exchange of vows had happened for different reasons.

"You're rather introspective tonight," she noted.

"Sorry," he said. "I was just making a mental list of a few last things that I need to pick up at the hardware store on the way home."

"Does *a few last things* mean that the renovation is almost complete?"

He nodded. "Fingers crossed, you'll be able to see the completed project on Saturday."

"You've made a lot of progress in two weeks, then," she said.

"I had a powerful incentive."

Regan smiled. "I can't wait to see it."

"You really haven't checked on the progress at all?"

He found it hard to believe that she hadn't even peeked when she'd come by the house, as she'd done a few times, to take Baxter for walks in the middle of the day. He had all entrances to the kitchen area blocked off with plastic to keep the dust and debris contained, but it would be easy enough to pull back the plastic and take a look. He'd taken pictures to document the progress, but she'd insisted that she didn't want to see those, either, until after.

She shook her head now in response to his question. "I was tempted," she admitted. "But I decided I'd rather wait."

"Well, I think you're going to be pleased. And Baxter is going to be so excited when you come home—the house has been so empty without you."

"Remember you said that," Regan teased. "Because we'll all likely be tripping over one another when your brother comes home."

"It won't be so bad," Connor said. "Especially as he has a full-time job for the summer."

"Where's he going to be working?"

"At Katelyn Davidson's law office."

"That's great," she said.

Her enthusiasm seemed genuine, prompting him to ask, "You don't mind that he's going to be spending his days with your archenemy."

"Archenemy?" she echoed, amused. "Am I a comic book character now?"

"Hmm...now that you mention it, I wouldn't mind seeing you in a spandex jumpsuit."

"Not going to happen," she assured him.

"Disappointing," he said. "But I was only referring to the history between the Blakes and the Gilmores."

"There's some bad blood there, as a result of which I can't imagine ever being best friends with a Gilmore," Regan acknowledged. "But it has nothing to do with me or Katelyn, even if she was a Gilmore before she married the sheriff."

"What about your sister and Liam?" he asked.

She seemed taken aback by the question. "Why would you ask that?"

"The way she reacted to the mention of his name when you were talking about the inn, I got the impression there might be some history there."

"No." She shook her head. "There's no history between Brie and Liam."

"Brie and Caleb, then," he guessed.

"So when is Deacon coming home?" she asked.

It was hardly a subtle effort to shift the topic of conversation, but Connor obliged. "His last exam is May ninth, and he flies back on the tenth."

"I'm sure he's eager to get home."

"And excited to meet his nieces," Connor told her.

"I'm glad you think so," Regan said. "Because I was hoping we could ask him to be Piper and Poppy's godfather."

"Really?"

She nodded. "Brie was the obvious choice for god-mother, because she's my only sister, and since Deacon is your only brother, well, it just made sense to me. What do you think?"

"I think it's a great idea," he agreed.

"Then the next order of business is to actually schedule a date for the baptism."

"You can work that out with your sister," he said. "Just tell me when and where."

She nodded. "And you should be forewarned—my parents have already said they'd like to have a party here after the event."

"You say that as if you expect me to object," he noted.

"I just thought we should do something for our daughters at our house."

"Which I wouldn't object to, either," he assured her. "But your parents have a lot more space—especially if the party had to be moved indoors."

"They also have Celeste," she realized.

"Well, yeah."

"I think she's the real reason you want to have the party here, because you know she'll be in charge of the food."

"That might have been a consideration," he allowed.

She grinned. "In which case I will say, you're a very smart man, Connor Neal."

"What's going on here?" Regan asked, sidling between a vacant stool at the bar and the one upon which her husband was seated.

It was Friday—the day before the big unveiling he'd promised—so she'd been understandably surprised to get the call from the owner of Diggers' Bar & Grill revealing that Connor was at the bar. Duke had asked if she could pick up her husband because he was in no condition to drive home and he didn't trust the deputy would be able to find his way if he walked.

"We're shelebrating."

She looked pointedly from the empty stool on her side to the trio of vacant seats on his other side. "We?"

"Well, everyone elsh is gone now."

Duke carried a steaming carafe of coffee over to top up the cup on the bar in front of Connor.

"He didn't have a lot to drink," the bartender said, shaking his head. "I've never known a grown man who was such a lightweight."

"How much isn't a lot?" she asked.

"Two beers, and then a couple of shots. It was the shots that seemed to do him in."

"Well, you said it," agreed Regan. "He's not much of a drinker."

And knowing that he grew up with a stepfather who got angry and belligerent when he was drunk, she understood why.

She turned her attention back to her husband. "What were you celebrating?"

"Kowalshki's gettin' married."

"That's happy news—and a good reason to celebrate," Regan acknowledged.

"Everyone was goin' for drinks," he explained. "I couldn't say no."

"Of course not," she agreed. "Though next time you might want to say no to the shots."

"Damn Shack Daniels."

She bit back a smile and looked at the bartender again. "Has he paid his tab?"

"Sheriff took care of it," Duke said.

She nodded and nudged her hip against Connor's thigh. "Let's get you home."

He put his feet on the ground, then reached out to grasp the edge of the bar to steady himself.

"You are a lightweight, aren't you?" she mused.

"Tired," he said. "Didn't sleep mush last night. Wanted to get the kitshen done."

She took his arm to guide him to the door. "Is it done?"

He nodded. "Celeste gave me a reshipee so I could make dinner for you tomorrow."

"A nice idea," she said, touched that he would want to cook the first meal for her in the new kitchen. "But maybe we should wait and see how hungover you are in the morning before we make any plans."

"You can come home now," he said.

"I'm taking you home right now," she promised, opening the passenger-side door of her SUV for him.

He folded himself into the seat, then turned to look behind him. "Where's the girls?"

"At my parents' place."

"Your parents are lookin' after them?"

She snorted. "I'd have to be drunker than you are to let that happen."

He frowned, clearly not understanding.

"Celeste is looking after them."

"Ahh." He nodded. "Celeste took care of you when you were a baby."

"Celeste still takes care of me—of all of us," Regan said.

"I wish we had a Celeste."

"My parents offered to pay her salary and have her help us out for a year," she reminded him.

"Your father thinks he can buy anything...or anyone."

She frowned at the bitter edge underlying the muttered words. "What are you talking about?"

"Nothin'."

"It sounded like something to me."

But he'd closed his eyes, and he didn't say anything else until they were almost home. "I have a 'feshun to make."

She turned into the driveway. "Is it something you're going to regret telling me when you're sober?" she wondered.

"I didn't jus' marry you to give your babies a father," he confided.

She turned off the ignition. "So why did you marry me?"

"I've hadda crush on you sinch high shcool."

"High school?" she echoed, surprised. "We barely knew each other in high school."

"You don't remember." He slapped a hand against his chest. "I'm wounded."

"I have no doubt your head is going to feel wounded in the morning," she told him. "But what is it you think I don't remember?"

"Twelfth grade calculus."

She got out of the car and went around to the passenger side to help him do the same. "I remember," she assured him. "I tutored you during lunch period on Tuesdays and Thursdays, and sometimes after school on Wednesdays."

"I got an A. Well, an A-minus, acshally, but I figured it counted."

"I know. You offered to take me out for ice cream to celebrate."

He nodded, paying careful attention to the steps as he climbed them. "But you had plans with Brett Tanner. Goin' to see 'Bill & Ted's Exshellent Avenshure.'"

She paused with her key in the lock. "How could you possibly remember such a trivial detail after so many years?"

"I hated Brett Tanner," he said. "Or maybe I jus' hated that you liked him."

She opened the door and hit the light switch inside.

Baxter, waiting—as always—on the other side of the door, gave a happy bark and danced around them in circles.

Regan fussed over the dog for a minute while Connor struggled to take off his boots. When he'd finally accomplished that task, she followed him up the stairs.

Apparently he'd resumed sleeping in the master bedroom after she'd gone, because he headed in that direction and collapsed on top of the mattress.

"Don't fall asleep just yet," she warned.

"'kay."

She went across the hall to the bathroom, returning with a cup of water and a couple of Tylenol. "Sit up and take these."

He eased himself into sitting position against the headboard. She dropped the tablets in his hand, then gave him the cup. He tossed back the pills and drank down the water.

She took the empty cup back to the bathroom and refilled it, then set it on the table beside the bed.

"Are you going to get under those covers or sleep on top of them?" she asked.

"You sleep with me?"

"Not tonight," she said. "I need to get back to our babies."

"Pretty babies," he said. "Jus' like their mama."

"You're talkative when you're drunk," she mused. "I'll have to remember that."

"I don't get drunk," he denied. "No more'n two beers—" he held up two fingers and squinted at them as if he wasn't quite sure it was the right number "—ever."

"You should have told that to your pal Shack Daniels."

He shook his head. "Not my pal."

She really did need to get back to Piper and Poppy, but she was curious about something he'd said earlier. She perched on the edge of the mattress and said, "What does your high school crush have to do with your proposal?"

"I finally got the mos' pop'lar girl in shcool to go out with me."

"I wasn't the most popular girl," she denied. "In fact, I hardly dated in high school." Because even as a teenager, she'd been focused on getting into a good college and earning a degree so that she could go to work with her parents at Blake Mining.

"You were tight with Brett Tanner."

"Not as tight as he wanted people to think," she confided.

"It doesn' matter. You lived in one of the biggest houses in town…an' I was a loser from the wrong shide of the tracks."

"You were never a loser," she said, shocked that he could ever have thought so little of himself. "And that expression—the wrong side of the tracks—never made any sense to me. Especially considering that the trains stopped running through Haven more than fifty years ago."

"But people still 'member where they ran."

"For what it's worth, I thought you were kind of cute back in high school," she confided.

"Cute?" he echoed.

"All my friends did, too," she told him.

"Cute?" he said again, as if the word was somehow distasteful.

"But in an edgy kind of way," she said. "Of course, bad boys have always been the downfall of good girls."

"An' you were the goodest of the good girls, weren't you?"

"I was a rule follower," she acknowledged. "Most of the time, anyway."

"When have you not followed the rules?" he wondered.

"My first date with you."

His brow furrowed, as if he was struggling to remember. "The wedding chapel in Reno?"

She nodded. "Getting married was the craziest thing I'd ever done on a first date."

"Prob'ly mine, too."

"Only probably?"

"I'm a bad boy, 'member?"

She took the throw from the rocking chair and draped it over him. "You keep telling yourself that."

"But it was defin'ly—" his eyes drifted shut "—my best first date ever."

She waited until she was sure he was asleep, then she leaned over and touched her lips to his forehead. "Mine, too."

"You don't look any the worse for wear," Regan remarked when Connor came outside to greet her the next day.

"I figured it was too much to hope that you'd let me forget about last night."

"Actually, I'm curious to know how much you remember."

"All of it." He opened the back door of her SUV and reached inside to unclip Piper's car seat, then he went around to the other side and did the same to Poppy's. "I think. After a handful of Tylenol and a gallon of water this morning, my head stopped pounding enough for the memories to become clearer."

She hefted the diaper bag onto her shoulder and followed him into the house.

Baxter could barely contain his excitement when Connor took the babies into the house. Although Regan had brought the twins with her when she came to take him for his walks, he seemed to sense that this time was different—that they were finally home—and he was in doggy heaven.

"But thank you," Connor said to her now. "Although I'm fairly confident I could have found my own way home last night, I appreciate you coming to get me."

"It was my pleasure," she said.

His gaze narrowed. "And now I'm wondering if there are some gaps in my memory."

"Maybe I'm just happy to be home," she told him. "And eager to see the new kitchen."

"Then I won't make you wait any longer," he said, leading the way.

She'd seen the plans, of course, so she had a general idea of what to expect. She'd approved of the floor tile and cabinet style and granite he'd chosen, but the mental image she'd pieced together in her mind didn't do justice to the final result.

"This is incredible," she said, gliding her fingertips along the beveled edge of the countertop. She opened a cupboard, appreciating the smooth movement of the hinge, and smiled when she saw that the new dishes she'd ordered were stacked neatly inside.

But not all of them.

Two place settings had been set out on the island,

with the shiny new cutlery set on top of sunny-yellow napkins. A bouquet of daffodils was stuffed into a clear vase in the corner.

"You do good work, Deputy."

He looked pleased with the compliment.

"And—do I smell something cooking?"

He nodded. "Chicken with roasted potatoes. Celeste promised it was a foolproof recipe, so if it doesn't taste as good as hers, I'm blaming the new oven."

"Don't you mean she promised it was a foolproof re-shipee?" she teased.

He shook his head. "Are you ever going to let me forget about last night?"

"I won't say another word."

But truthfully, she didn't want to forget about last night—or at least not about the revelation he'd made. Because if it was true that he'd had a crush on her in high school, maybe it wasn't outside the realm of possibility that he might develop real feelings for her now. As she'd developed real feelings for him.

And then maybe, someday, their marriage of convenience would become something more.

Chapter Fourteen

Every detail of The Stagecoach Inn reflected elegance and indulgence, and excited butterflies winged around inside Regan's belly as she checked in at the double pedestal desk. After the formalities were taken care of, she'd been invited to a wine and cheese reception for guests in the library, but she'd opted to explore the main lobby on her own while she waited for her husband to arrive.

She glanced at her watch. 5:58.

Connor was supposed to meet her at six o'clock, but because she'd gotten there early, she'd spent the last twelve minutes pretending she wasn't watching the time. She thought about taking a leisurely stroll down the street, to distract herself for a few minutes, but she didn't trust Connor to wait if he showed up at six o'clock and she wasn't there.

Instead she perched on the edge of a butter leather sofa facing the stone fireplace and pulled her phone out of her pocket to send a brief text message to her sister.

Maybe this was a bad idea.

Brie immediately replied:

Don't u dare chicken out!

I'm not chi

That was as far as she got in typing her reply before Connor stepped through the front door.

She tucked the phone back into her pocket and stood up.

"Hey." He smiled when he saw her, and the curve of his lips somehow managed to reassure her while also releasing a kaleidoscope of butterflies in her belly.

"What's going on?" he asked. "Where are Piper and Poppy?"

"They're at home with the babysitters."

His brows lifted. "We have babysitters?"

She nodded. "Alyssa and Jason thought looking after the twins would give them a crash course in parenting, to help prepare them for the arrival of their own baby."

"Okay, but why are we here?"

"Because it's our anniversary."

He frowned at that. "We got married in September."

"The twenty-sixth," she confirmed. "Which makes today our seven-month anniversary."

"I didn't know that was a thing," he said, sounding worried. "Was I supposed to get you a card? Send flowers?"

She shook her head. "I didn't get you anything, either. This—" she held up an antique key "—is a belated-wedding-slash-early-anniversary gift from my sister."

He swallowed. "She got us a hotel room?"

"The luxury suite," Regan clarified, taking his hand and leading him up the stairs toward their accommodations on the top floor.

"It's a nice idea," he acknowledged, his steps slowing as they approached the second-floor landing. "But…"

She nodded, understanding everything that was implied by that single word. But theirs wasn't a traditional marriage. It wasn't even a *real* marriage. Although she knew that Brie had booked the suite for them in an effort to change that.

"Just come and see the room," she urged.

She'd already checked in and been escorted to the suite by Liam Gilmore, the hotel's owner doing double-duty as bellhop. He'd given her a brief history of the hotel as they climbed to the upper level, a scripted speech that filled what would likely have been an awkward silence otherwise.

She might have made some appropriate comment when he was done, but then he opened the door of the suite and she'd been rendered speechless. The plaque on the wall beside the door identified Wild Bill's Getaway Suite, but everything inside the space screamed luxury and elegance.

The floor of the foyer was covered in an intricate pattern of mosaic tile; the walls were painted a pale shade of gold and set off by wide white trim. Beyond the foyer was a carpeted open-concept sitting area that Liam had called a parlor, with an antique-looking sofa and chaise lounge facing the white marble fireplace over which was mounted an enormous flat-screen TV. Beyond the parlor was the bath, with more white marble, lots of glass and shiny chrome and even a crystal chandelier. On the other side of the bath was the bedroom, which boasted a second fireplace—this one with a dark marble surround, a king-size pediment poster bed flanked by matching end tables, a wide wardrobe and a makeup vanity set with padded stool.

"This is...impressive," Connor said. Then, his tone almost apologetic, he added, "But we can't stay."

"Do you want to explain why to my sister, who pre-paid for two nights?" she asked.

"She knows you're nursing Piper and Poppy. It should

be simple enough to explain that you can't be away from them for two days."

"She also knows I've got a pump. And there's enough breast milk in the freezer at home for a week." She'd finally overcome her opposition to occasional bottle feeding after a visit from Macy Clayton—a single mom of triplets—who wanted to reassure Regan that there were other "moms of multiples" out there who could be a great resource when she had questions or concerns about raising her twins. (Coincidentally, Macy was also the manager of the Stagecoach Inn—and dating Liam Gilmore.) Macy had urged Regan not to demand too much of herself and suggested that if her husband was willing to give a baby a bottle, she should let him—and not feel guilty but grateful.

"What about Baxter?"

"Jason promised to walk him twice a day. I even mapped out Baxter's usual route for him."

"But all I've got are the clothes on my back."

"I packed a bag for you," she said. "It's in the bedroom."

"I guess that shoots down all my arguments," Connor acknowledged, sounding more resigned than pleased at the prospect of being alone with his wife.

And Regan was suddenly assailed by doubts, too.

Being married was both easier and harder than she'd anticipated when she'd accepted the deputy's impulsive proposal.

It was easier because Connor had truly become her partner in parenting Piper and Poppy. He obviously adored the two little girls—and the feeling was mutual. Their faces lit up whenever he walked into a room and they happily snuggled against his broad chest to fall asleep, assuring Regan that she couldn't have chosen a better father for her children.

And it was harder because of the deep affection and growing attraction she felt for her husband. She'd agreed to marry Connor because she'd been alone and scared. She hadn't worried that she might fall in love with her husband. In fact, she would have scoffed at the very idea that she could.

But over the past seven months, her awareness had grown and her feelings had changed, and she was hoping that his had, too. However, if she'd harbored any illusions that Connor would be overcome by desire when he found himself in a romantic hotel suite with his wife, his lukewarm response quickly dispelled them.

"Maybe we should go out to grab a bite to eat," he suggested to her now.

"We could go down to The Home Station," she said. "Unless you'd rather have something sent up here?"

"I heard it's next to impossible to get a table in the restaurant."

"Mostly because priority is given to hotel guests," she explained. "When I checked in, they told me to call down to the desk if we wanted to make a reservation."

"Then we should take advantage of that," he decided.

"Or we could take advantage of this luxurious suite," she suggested. "Because the restaurant menu is also available through room service."

He didn't take the hint. "But the restaurant is closer to the kitchen, so the food will be hotter and fresher when it gets to a table down there."

It sounded like a reasonable argument. And it was possible that he wasn't deliberately being obtuse but was simply hungry. Wasn't it?

"In that case, why don't you call down to the desk for a reservation while I go freshen up?" she said.

"Okay," he agreed, sounding relieved.

While he reached for the phone, Regan retreated to the bedroom.

She opened up her suitcase, trying to remember if she'd packed something suitable for a fancy dinner. Truthfully, she hadn't worried too much about what she'd thrown into the case, optimistic that she wasn't going to need a lot of clothes over the next couple of days. She'd been more concerned about ensuring that she had all necessary personal items—including the box of condoms that she'd bought in hopeful anticipation of finally consummating their marriage.

Was she being too subtle? Or was Connor simply not interested? Over the past few weeks, he'd sent so many mixed signals she could hardly figure which way was up. One day he was kissing her senseless, the next he was moving her out of his house. While she was gone, he could hardly stay away from her, but since her return, he'd gone back to sleeping in his brother's room.

Of course, that escape wouldn't be available to him for much longer. Deacon was studying for his final exams now and would be on his way home soon. But that was little consolation to Regan, who didn't want Connor to share her bed out of necessity but choice, and she hated that he seemed to want an escape.

The television came on in the other room.

With a resigned sigh, Regan picked up her phone again and sent another text to her sister.

I'm about to chicken out.

She waited for Brie to reply—and nearly dropped the phone when it rang in her hand.

"Don't you dare," her sister said without preamble when Regan connected the call.

"It's just…maybe it's too soon."

"You've been married seven months," Brie reminded her. "Or do you mean too soon after the babies? Because I thought you said the doctor gave you the thumbs-up."

"She did," Regan confirmed.

"So what's your hesitation?"

"I'm not sure," she admitted. "It just seems like a big step."

"It *is* a big step," her sister agreed.

"And if we have sex…it's going to change everything."

"Don't you want things to change?"

"Some things," she acknowledged.

"Such as the fact that you're not having sex with your husband?"

She sighed. "Okay, yes. But we've actually got a pretty good relationship otherwise."

"Just think about how much better it will be when you add naked fun to the mix," her sister urged.

"Maybe that's the part that's holding me back," she said.

"You're opposed to having fun?" Brie teased.

"I meant the naked part," Regan clarified.

"Well, it's been a long time since I've had sex," her sister offered. "But as I recall, it's easier without clothes on."

"You seem to be forgetting that I had two babies four and a half weeks ago."

"I'm not forgetting anything. The whole point of getting you out of the house was to ensure that my adorable nieces wouldn't put a damper on your love life—at least not this weekend."

"The babies have hardly put a damper on our love life," Regan assured her.

"Only because you don't have one…yet."

"I guess that's what I get for telling you the truth," she muttered.

"Or at least part of the truth."

"What do you think I left out?"

"How much you care about your husband," Brie suggested.

"Of course I care about him," Regan said.

"And that you're seriously attracted to him," her sister added.

"He's a good man with a lot of attractive qualities," she admitted.

"And a smokin'-hot body," Brie noted.

That gave her pause. "You checked out my husband?"

"I needed to be sure he was worthy of my sister."

Regan sighed. "What am I going to do?"

"Your smokin'-hot husband?" her sister suggested.

She choked on a laugh. "If only it were that simple."

"It's only complicated because you're making it complicated," Brie insisted.

"We're in a seriously fancy hotel room and I'm on the phone with my sister while he's watching TV in another room."

"I'm sure, if you put your mind to it, you could make him forget about whatever was on the screen—even if he was a diehard football fan and it was Super Bowl Sunday," Brie said. "But if you need a little confidence boost, look inside the drawer of the bedside table."

Curious, she tugged open the drawer and found a lingerie-size box wrapped in pink-striped paper. The tag attached read:

For Regan (& Connor)—Enjoy! Love, Brie XO

"Is it sexy or slutty?" she asked.

Brie laughed. "A little of both. Now go put it on—

and I don't want to hear from you again until the weekend's over."

With that, her sister disconnected.

Regan stared at the package for a long minute, debating.

Brie had gone to a lot of effort to make this weekend special for her sister and brother-in-law, so Regan decided that she could at least do her part.

Connor had thought the first seven months of his marriage to Regan—living in close proximity but not being able to touch her—had been torturous enough. He suspected the next forty-eight hours were going to make those seven months seem like a walk in the park.

While she was in the bedroom, he'd checked to see if the sofa in the sitting area folded out to a bed. It did. But even if it didn't, he figured that squeezing his six-foot-four-inch frame into a five-foot sofa would likely be easier than trying to keep his hands off Regan if they were sharing a bed.

But maybe she didn't expect him to keep his hands to himself. Maybe she wanted to celebrate their anniversary the way most other couples celebrated anniversaries—naked together. Certainly she hadn't seemed the least bit reluctant to show him around the suite—including the luxurious bedroom dominated by the fancy bed. She might have been a little apprehensive if she'd known it had taken more willpower than he'd thought he possessed not to throw her down on top of that enormous mattress and have his way with her. Because he'd imagined a lot of various and interesting ways over the past seven months.

But Piper and Poppy were barely four weeks old, which meant that it would be another two before her body would be recovered enough from the experience of childbirth to engage in intercourse.

The longest six weeks of my life, Reid had remarked, in apparent sympathy with his deputy.

Of course, there were a lot of ways to share physical intimacy and sexual pleasure aside from sex. But Connor also knew that six weeks was only a guideline, that some women required a lot more time than that before they experienced any sexual desire.

He'd turned on the TV in a desperate effort to distract himself from the tantalizing thought that they were alone in a hotel room—at least until they could escape to the restaurant for their eight o'clock dinner reservation.

"Connor?"

"Hmm?" he said, his gaze fixed on the TV as he feigned interest in the action on the screen, though he couldn't have said if it was a movie or a commercial or a public service announcement.

Regan stepped forward then, so that she was standing directly in front of him, and his jaw nearly hit the floor.

The remote did slip from his hand and fall to the soft carpet.

He didn't notice.

He didn't see anything but Regan.

She was wearing something that could only be described as a fantasy of white satin and sheer lace. The lace cups barely covered the swell of her luscious breasts; the short skirt skimmed the tops of her creamy thighs.

He lifted his gaze to her face and swallowed. "I thought you were getting ready to go out for dinner."

"I decided that I don't want to go out for dinner."

"That's good," he said. "Because you'd start a riot if you walked into the restaurant wearing that."

She tilted her head to study him. "I can't tell if that means you approve or disapprove."

"Do you want my approval?"

"I want to know if you want *me*."

"Only more than I want to breathe," he admitted hoarsely.

Her glossy pink lips curved as she moved closer. "That's just the right amount," she said, as she straddled his hips with her knees and lowered herself into his lap.

The position put her breasts, practically spilling out of her top and rising and falling with every breath she took, right there at eye level. But he wanted to do more than just look.

He wanted to touch, taste, take.

Instead, he curled his fingers around the edge of the sofa cushion, desperately trying to hold on to the last vestiges of his self-control, but it was rapidly falling away like a slippery thread.

She leaned closer, so that her mouth was only a whisper from his, and he was about half a second from losing his mind.

But instead of touching her lips to his, she touched them to his cheek, then his jaw and his throat. Light brushes that teased and tempted.

His hands gripped the leather cushion tighter.

"Six weeks," he said hoarsely.

She lifted her head, her eyes dark with desire and sparkling with playfulness. "What?"

"It hasn't been six weeks."

She laughed softly and nipped at the lobe of his ear. "Six weeks is only a guideline, not a rule," she told him.

"You're sure?" he asked.

Please be sure.

She nodded. "I saw Dr. Amaro on Tuesday."

He exhaled an audible sigh of relief. "Thank you, Dr. Amaro."

"Your sentiment is noted," she said. "But I'd prefer you to focus on me right now."

"I can do that," he promised.

And in one abrupt and agile motion, Connor rose to his feet, taking her with him.

Chapter Fifteen

Regan yelped in surprise; Connor responded with a chuckle. One of his arms was banded around her waist while the opposite hand cupped her bottom, and though she didn't think she was in any danger of falling, she wrapped her arms and legs around him like a pretzel and held on.

He carried her to the bedroom and tumbled with her onto the mattress, pinning her beneath his lean, hard body. Her heart hammered against her ribs, not with fear but desire. Desperate, achy desire.

He eased back to hook his fingers in the satin straps of her baby doll, pulling them down her arms so that her breasts spilled free of their constraint. But then he captured them in his hands, exploring their shape and texture with his callused palms and clever fingers. His thumbs traced lazy circles around her already taut nipples, making everything inside her clench in eager anticipation.

"It's been torture, sleeping next to you night after night, not being able to touch you like this," he said.

"No one said you couldn't touch me like this," she pointed out.

"Well, it seemed to be implied that there were... boundaries...to our relationship."

"Tonight, let's forget about the boundaries," she suggested.

"That sounds good to me," he said.

And then he was too busy kissing her to say anything more.

He was a really good kisser: his mouth was firm but not hard; his tongue bold but not aggressive. At another time, she thought she could happily spend hours kissing and being kissed by him. But after so many months of wanting and waiting, it wasn't enough. She wanted more.

As if sensing her impatience, he eased his mouth from hers, skimming it over her jaw, down her throat. He traced the line of her collarbone with his tongue, then nuzzled the hollow between her breasts. His shadowed jaw rasped against her tender flesh, like the strike of a match. Then his mouth found her nipple, and the shocking contrast of his hot mouth on her cool skin turned the spark to flame. He licked and suckled, making her gasp and yearn.

Oh, how she yearned.

As his mouth continued to taste and tease, his hands slid under the hem of her nightie to tug her panties over her hips and down her legs. He tossed the scrap of lace aside and nudged her thighs apart. His thumbs glided over the slick flesh at her core, parting the folds, zeroing in on the center of her feminine pleasure.

Was it post-childbirth hormones running rampant through her system that were responsible for the escalation in her desire, the intensity of her response? Or was it finally being with Connor as she'd so often dreamed of being with him?

Had he dreamed of her, too? Had he imagined touching her the way he was touching her now? Or did he just instinctively know where and how to use his hands so that she couldn't help but sigh with exquisite pleasure?

She should have guessed that he'd approach lovemaking the same way he did everything else—thoroughly and with great attention to detail. But she wanted to touch him, too, so she yanked his shirt out of his pants and made quick work of the buttons.

She finally managed to shove the garment aside and put her hands on him. The taut muscles of his belly quivered as she trailed her fingers over his torso; a low groan emanated from his throat as she scraped her nails lightly down his back. When she reached for his belt, he pulled away to assist with the task—quickly discarding his pants, briefs and socks in a pile on the floor.

"Condom," she said, when he rejoined her on the bed.

It was widely accepted that nursing moms couldn't get pregnant, but with four-and-a-half-week-old twins at home, she didn't want to take any chances.

He reached for the square packet she'd set on top of the bedside table in anticipation of this moment, and quickly sheathed himself.

His eyes were dark and intently focused as he rose over her again.

"I feel as if I've been waiting for this moment forever," he confided. "I don't want to rush it now."

"And I don't want to wait a second longer."

His lips curved as they brushed against hers. "Demanding, much?"

But he gave her what she wanted—what they both wanted. In one smooth stroke, he buried himself deep inside her.

She cried out at the shock and pleasure of the invasion as he filled her, as new waves of sensation began to ripple through her. He held her hands above her head, their fingers entwined, then lowered his head and captured her mouth. She wrapped her legs around him, so that they were linked from top to toe and everywhere in between. Two bodies joined together in pursuit of their mutual pleasure…and finding it.

Regan awoke in the night, her breasts full and aching.

A quick glance at the clock beside the bed confirmed that it was 4 a.m. Poppy habitually woke up around 3:30 and Piper about half an hour later. The staggered times meant that each twin got individual attention, but it also meant that their mom spent twice as much time nursing. Regan knew that it was possible to nurse two babies at the same time, but she couldn't imagine ever being that coordinated—or able to sync their schedules.

She slipped out of bed, leaving Connor sleeping, and retreated to the bathroom with her breast pump. Her initial concerns about not being able to produce enough milk to satisfy the twins had proved to be for naught, and she'd left a more than adequate supply for the weekend in the freezer and detailed instructions for Alyssa about how to prepare it.

Regan was genuinely happy that Jason and Alyssa were starting a family. And that Spencer and Kenzie were expanding theirs. It was apparent that both of her brothers had fallen in love with their perfect mates. Not that either of them had followed a short or easy path to happily-ever-after, but they got there eventually.

Love hadn't been anywhere on Regan's radar when she'd exchanged vows with Connor at the little chapel in Reno. She'd been alone and scared—terrified of being a single mom to two babies, drowning in doubts and insecurities when he tossed her a lifeline in the form of his proposal. She'd snatched it up desperately, gratefully, never hoping or even imagining that their marriage of convenience would ever become anything more.

But over the past seven and a half months, her feelings for her husband had changed and deepened so much so that she knew she was on the verge of falling in love with him.

Or maybe she'd already fallen.

There wasn't any one moment or factor she could pinpoint as the time or reason why, although she knew a big part of it was that she loved him for loving their babies. It took a special kind of man to step up and be a dad in the absence of any biological connection to the child, but Connor had never hesitated or wavered.

Regan knew he loved Piper and Poppy—the only question that remained was: could he ever love her?

The next time she awakened, sunlight was trying to peek around the edges of the curtain. Beneath her cheek, she could feel Connor's heart beating—a slow and steady rhythm. She idly wondered how long it would take her to get his heart racing again, like it had raced the night before.

Not long, was the answer, as he proved when he woke up only a few minutes later.

Regan had never been a big fan of morning sex, but as she'd begun to realize, everything was different with Connor.

Afterward, when she was snuggled close to him, she stroked a hand down the arm that was wrapped around her, following the contours of taut muscles. It amazed her that a man so physically strong could be so tender and gentle, as he'd proved last night and again only a short while ago.

"What happened here?" she asked, her fingers skimming over the vertical line of puckered skin that ran down his forearm.

He glanced at the jagged scar, almost as if he'd forgotten it was there. "Broken glass."

"What'd you do? Put your arm through a window?"

"No."

"Did it happen on the job?" she prompted, when he offered no further explanation.

"No," he said again, adding a shake of his head this time. "It was a long time ago."

"How long?" she asked curiously.

"Ten…maybe twelve…years ago."

She was surprised and dismayed by the result of the quick mental calculation. "When you were a teenager?"

"Yeah."

Another single syllable response, but she refused to be dissuaded. "I know we're both adjusting to the new parameters of our marriage, but I believe communication is key to the success of any relationship."

"Words aren't the only means of communication," he said, with a suggestive wiggle of his brows.

"Yes, and you've proven that you're quite adept at other forms of communication," she assured him. "So if you don't want to talk about it, just say so."

"And you'll let it go?" he asked dubiously.

"Probably not," she admitted. "I can be like Baxter with a juicy T-bone when I want to know something."

He chuckled. "Yeah, that's what I figured." His expression grew serious as he looked at the scar on his arm again. "Do you know Mallory Stillwell?"

"The name sounds vaguely familiar," she admitted, already second-guessing her decision to push for an explanation. She'd thought she wanted to know everything about him, but she hadn't anticipated that his answer might involve another woman.

"She grew up in my neighborhood," he explained. "Across the street and two doors down."

"You took her to prom," Regan suddenly remembered.

"Only because Dale Shillington ditched her two days before the event and she was devastated about not being able to go—especially after she'd worked three weekends of overtime shifts at Jo's to buy a new dress."

"Dale Shillington always was a dick."

"I won't argue with that," Connor said.

"So you stepped in to help out a…friend?" she asked, blatantly fishing for more information about the nature of her husband's relationship with the girl-almost-next-door.

"We were friends," he confirmed. "And, for a while, we were more."

"You can spare me those details," she said quickly.

"I wasn't planning on sharing them."

Which she should have realized. Connor had never been the type to kiss and tell—which only made her that much more curious.

"And you went to prom with Brett Tanner that year," he noted.

"Because he asked."

"You wore a black dress," he said. "All the other girls were in shades of pink or purple or blue, heavy on the makeup and tottering around on too-high heels as if playing at being grown-up. Then you walked in—in your black dress with skinny straps and long skirt, and you were so straight-up sexy, you took my breath away."

"That's quite the memory," she remarked, embarrassed to admit that she couldn't summon an image of him at prom. She knew he'd been there, because she'd heard the stories that circulated, not just that night but for several weeks afterward, but it was possible she hadn't actually seen him.

"You made quite the impression," he assured her.

"And you got kicked out," she said, as her hazy memories slowly came into focus.

"What else would anyone expect from that no-good Neal boy?"

"Did you ever really do anything to earn that reputation?"

"I got kicked out of prom," he reminded her.

"What does any of this have to do with your scar?" she asked, in an effort to steer the conversation back on topic.

"Like my stepfather, Mallory's mom was a heavy drinker—and a mean drunk. And when she'd been drinking, she liked to knock her kids around. Mallory, being the oldest, usually took the brunt of the abuse."

Regan's fingers skimmed down his arm again, over the jagged scar, to link with his.

"One day she went at Mallory with a broken bottle and I stepped between them—and got thirty-four stitches for my efforts."

She winced, not wanting to imagine the bloody scene. "Was she arrested?"

He shook his head. "Mallory begged me to say that it was an accident."

"Why?"

"Because if her mother had gone to jail, family services would have come in and taken her sisters away."

"Considering their mother's violent abuse, that might have been better for them," she remarked.

"Says the girl born with a silver spoon in her mouth."

She nudged him away. "You're going to hold that against me?"

He shook his head. "No, I'm just pointing out why you can't understand the realities of life for those of us who grew up without the same privileges."

"You don't think Mallory and her sisters would have been better off in a different environment?"

"Maybe," he allowed. "Except that no one worried too much about separating siblings back then, and that might have been even more traumatic for all of them."

"I never thought about that," she admitted.

"And I don't want you thinking—and worrying—about it now," he said. "I just wanted to give you a complete picture."

"Got it."

"Good. Now can we stop talking about ex-girlfriends and high school and focus on the here and now?" he suggested, rolling over so that he was facing her.

"What, exactly, in the here and now do you want to focus on?"

"I'd like to start here," he said, and nibbled on her throat.

Her head dropped back and a sigh slipped between her lips. "That's a good place to start," she agreed.

"And here," he said, skimming his lips along the underside of her jaw.

"Another good place."

As his mouth continued to taste and tease, his hands moved lower. A quick tug unknotted the belt at her waist, and the silky robe fell open. She immediately tried to draw the sides together again, but he caught her wrists and held them in place.

"Why are you suddenly acting shy?"

"Because you opened the curtains and it's broad daylight."

"We're on the third floor. No one can see in," he told her.

"But you can see me," she protested.

"That was the point," he said. "I want to see and touch and taste every part of you."

"Some of those parts aren't as firm or smooth as they used to be."

"All of your parts are perfect." He brushed his lips over hers. "You're perfect."

She wasn't, of course. But it was nice of him to say so, and to sound as if he really believed it.

She'd had several boyfriends and a few lovers, but she'd always been careful to keep them at an emotional distance. She enjoyed sex but was wary of messy emotional entanglements. She hadn't been able to keep Connor at a distance. Or maybe she hadn't wanted to.

"What are you thinking about?"

"I was just wondering...do you think we can make our marriage work?"

"I think we've been doing a pretty good job of it so far," he pointed out. "And that was without the added benefits of sex."

"I guess I just worry sometimes—"

"You worry all the time," he interjected.

She managed a small smile. "Well, sometimes I worry that you might wake up one day and regret marrying me."

He shook his head. "Never."

"How can you be so sure?"

"Because I love the life we have together," he said.

It wasn't a declaration of feelings for her, but she decided it was close enough—at least for now.

"I'm really glad you were there when I was puking in the bushes outside of Diggers'," she said softly.

He chuckled and brushed his lips over her temple. "Me, too."

Chapter Sixteen

Two weeks after their weekend at The Stagecoach Inn—two weeks during which he'd continued to enjoy the many benefits of sharing a bed with his wife at home—Connor drove to the airport in Elko to pick up his brother. For a lot of years, it had been just him and Deacon, and it had been a big adjustment for both of them when his brother went away to school.

It wasn't just that Deacon was gone, but that he was so far away, and the cost of travel meant that he'd only been home once in the past eight months. And when he'd made that trip at Christmas, Connor hadn't been able to relax and enjoy his brother's company because Deacon's presence meant he had to move back into his own room, occupied by an incredibly sexy and far-too-tempting woman who just happened to be his wife.

This time there was no similar apprehension about Deacon's homecoming, just anticipation for the chance to reconnect with his only sibling.

The first night, after Deacon had finally been introduced to his nieces and made a suitable fuss over "the cutest babies ever"—and then an equal fuss over Baxter, reassuring the dog that he was also loved and adored—they stayed up late talking. Regan lasted until ten o'clock, explaining to her brother-in-law that Piper and Poppy didn't just get up early but continued to wake a couple of times through the night.

"I didn't say it at Christmas, because I was still trying to wrap my head around the fact that you were married," Deacon said, after his brother's wife had gone upstairs. "But I'm really happy for you and Regan."

"Thanks," Connor said.

"And I think it's pretty cool that I'm an uncle—times two."

"With twins, everything is times two," Connor told him. "Twice as many feedings and dirty diapers and loads of laundry."

"Twice as much cuteness," his brother added. "Of course, that's only because they look so much like their mom."

"Lucky for them," Connor agreed.

And lucky for him, because if Piper and Poppy didn't look so much like Regan, people might start to wonder why they didn't look anything at all like their dad.

"Seriously, though, those kids are lucky they've got you for a dad," Deacon remarked.

"I'm the fortunate one," he said. "When I married Regan, I got everything I never knew I wanted."

"She seems pretty great," his brother acknowledged. "I have to admit, when I first got the letter about my scholarship, I didn't realize that it was my sister-in-law's family that was responsible for the fund."

"Blake Mining throws a ton of money around," Connor told him, attempting to downplay the familial connection. "Probably in the hope of some positive PR to combat the negative environmental impact of the business."

"So Regan didn't pull any strings to get me the scholarship?" Deacon asked, wanting to be sure.

"I promise that she didn't," Connor said.

Because Deacon returned to Haven in the middle of the week, he had a few days off before he was scheduled to start working at Katelyn Davidson's law office the following Monday. Unfortunately, Connor didn't have any of those days off. Not even the weekend, because it was his turn in the rotation.

"I know it sucks that it's your first week back and your brother's hardly been home," Regan said to him, after a leisurely breakfast Saturday morning.

"We'll have plenty of time to catch up over the summer," Deacon said. "And I've kind of enjoyed hanging out with you and Piper and Poppy. And Baxter," he added, with a glance at the dog sprawled by his feet.

"I was worried that you might feel uncomfortable, coming home to a place where so much has changed."

"You mean because I came back at Christmas and met my brother's wife? Then, four months later, when I finished the school term, there were two babies in the house?"

"Something like that," she agreed.

"There have been a lot of changes," he acknowledged. "But all for the better."

"I'm glad you think so."

"It's good to see Connor happy," Deacon said. "Not that he ever seemed unhappy, but he smiles a lot more now. Laughs more.

"I have to be honest, I wasn't sure he'd ever want to take on the roles of husband and father. It was pretty rough for him," he explained. "Growing up without a father."

"I doubt it was any rougher than you growing up with yours," Regan said gently.

He seemed startled by her remark. "He told you about Dwayne?"

She nodded.

"I don't really remember much about him. Or maybe

I don't want to remember much, because what I do remember—" He cut himself off with a shake of his head.

"Anyway, it was Connor who mostly raised me," he continued. "Despite the fact that there's only eight years between us, he was the closest thing I had to a father. My own was useless on a good day, and our mom was always working.

"It was Connor who made sure I had clean clothes and a lunch packed for school. He filled out the trip forms and gave me milk money from his own savings."

"He never told me any of that," Regan admitted.

"He's always been the first one to step up to help someone else and the last one to want any credit for his actions," Deacon said.

She nodded, agreeing with his assessment.

"Do you know why I applied to Columbia?" Deacon asked.

"Because it's one of the top law schools in the country?" she suggested.

"Well, yeah," he acknowledged. "But I never actually planned to go there. Truthfully, I didn't even think I'd get in. But if I did, what an interesting story I'd have to tell the other lawyers in the barristers' lounge. Over single-malt scotch and imported cigars and conversations about our alma maters, I could casually mention that yes, I'd graduated from UNLV, but I could have gone to Columbia."

"You don't drink or smoke," she said, pointing out the obvious flaws in his story.

He chuckled. "In this futuristic scene of my imagination, I did. But Connor changed that futuristic scene for me. He changed that 'could have gone' to an 'am going.'"

"I know he's incredibly proud of you," she told him.

"And I'm incredibly grateful to him," Deacon said.

"How grateful?" Regan wondered.

"Uh-oh. That sounds like the prelude to a request for a big favor," he remarked.

"It is," she admitted. "Piper and Poppy's baptism is scheduled for June thirtieth and we'd like you to be a godparent."

A smile—quick and wide—spread across his face. "Me? No kidding?"

"No kidding," she assured him. "What do you say?"

"I'd be honored," he said. "But now I have a question for you."

"What is it?"

"What exactly is a godfather supposed to do —and does it include having to change stinky diapers?"

The middle of the following week, Piper and Poppy had their two-month checkup with their pediatrician in Battle Mountain.

"I appreciate the company on the drive," Regan said to Connor, when they headed back to the car with their healthy and happy baby girls after the appointment. "But you really don't have to come to every checkup with me."

"I know," he said. "But it's a long way for you to come on your own, especially if they start fussing. Plus, booking half a day off work gives me an excuse to take my wife out to lunch."

"Now that you mention it…I am kind of hungry."

"What are you in the mood for?"

"Pizza from Jo's," she decided.

"I thought you'd want to take advantage of the fact that we're in a town that offers a few more dining options than the Sunnyside Diner, Diggers' Bar and Grill, and Jo's Pizza."

"But if we pick up a pizza on the way home, I can

take advantage of my husband before he has to go into work later."

He grinned. "I like the way you think."

By the time they got around to eating the pizza, it was cold, but neither of them complained. After lunch, Regan wrapped the leftover slices while Connor went upstairs to get dressed.

She was startled when the doorbell rang, because Baxter was out in the backyard and hadn't given her any warning that someone was approaching the house. Although it was unusual to get visitors in the middle of the day, she was more curious than concerned when she responded to the summons.

Until she opened the door and discovered Bo Larsen on the other side.

"Hello, Regan."

There were at least a dozen random questions spinning through her mind, and she blurted out the first one she latched on to: "What are you doing here?"

"I was in town and thought I'd stop by to congratulate the new mother," he said.

Though the words sounded pleasant enough, she remained wary. "Thank you."

"You don't want to know who told me?"

"It's a small town and hardly a big secret," she pointed out.

"True," he acknowledged. "And it wasn't really a surprise to me, either. At least, not after I received a tax receipt for my generous donation to The Battle Mountain Women's Health Center.

"You can imagine how awkward it was," he continued in a conversational tone, "trying to explain that to my wife."

"I can," she agreed. "But I have to say, I approve of your philanthropy."

"Don't you mean *your* philanthropy?" he asked. "You took the money I gave you and turned it over to the clinic."

She didn't deny it. "You wanted to pay for an abortion, and I wasn't interested in having one."

"You might have told me that."

"Why? You made it perfectly clear that you had no interest in my baby."

"Don't you mean babies?"

She swallowed. "What do you want, Bo?"

"I just wanted to make sure—" His words cut off as his gaze shifted to focus on something—or someone, she guessed—over her shoulder.

"Everything okay?" Connor asked, as he came down the stairs to take up position behind her.

"Everything's fine," Regan said, breathing a silent sigh of relief that her husband wasn't carrying one or both of their daughters. "And Bo was just leaving."

"I don't want to rush off without being properly introduced to…" He paused, obviously waiting for her to fill in the blank.

"My husband," Regan told him. "Connor is my husband."

"Husband," Bo echoed, sounding surprised. "When we…worked together, I didn't get the impression that you were looking for a long-term commitment. But I guess parenthood changes a lot of things."

"Meeting the right person changes everything," Regan said pointedly.

Bo nodded. "Apparently so."

Regan turned to her husband then. "This is Bo Larsen, a former colleague."

"Oh, we were more than colleagues," he chided.

Regan narrowed her gaze.

Of course, Connor knew exactly what she and Bo had been. When she'd told him about her pregnancy, she'd told him everything. What he didn't know, because she'd only recently realized it herself, was that her relationship with Bo had been a mistake from the beginning.

And yet, even if she could go back in time, she wouldn't change a thing, because Bo was the reason she had Piper and Poppy—and they were the reason Connor had married her.

"We were also friends," her ex continued.

"And now we're not," she said pointedly.

Bo nodded. "I'm glad I got to meet your husband." He looked at Connor then. "Congratulations on your wedding. And your new family."

"Thank you," Connor said.

As soon as Bo turned away, Regan closed the door and turned the lock.

Connor stood behind her, watching Regan as she watched, through the glass, her former lover drive away. He could see the tension in the rigid line of her shoulders and practically feel it emanating from her body.

Did she want to be sure that he was gone?

Or was she wishing that he'd stayed?

"Are you okay?"

She turned around quickly and nodded. "I'm fine." She added a smile. "And reassured."

"Reassured?" he echoed dubiously.

She nodded again. "I always suspected he'd show up someday. Now that day has passed, and I don't have to worry that he'll come back again."

"How can you be sure?" he wondered.

"Because I saw how relieved he was to learn that we were married."

Connor hoped she was right and they'd seen the last of the other man. But even if it was true, that didn't eliminate the last of his concerns.

He hated to ask the question, but he needed to know: "Do you still have feelings for him?"

Regan shook her head. "Of course not. After the way he lied to me and used me? How could you even imagine that I would?"

"You said you knew he'd show up someday… I guess I just wondered if maybe that's why you made the donation to the women's health center in his name—to ensure that he would? To give him a reason to find you and force this confrontation?"

"No," she said again. "At the time, I was only thinking of getting rid of the money. Maybe I should have just torn up the check, but I was hurt and angry and obviously not thinking very clearly."

He wanted to believe it was as simple as that, but the other man's appearance at the door had shaken Connor more than he wanted to admit. He'd known about the relationship. She'd been honest with him about her former lover, but now that abstract persona had taken a specific form in a suit and tie, with a preppy haircut and neatly buffed nails.

Bo Larsen was exactly the type of guy he would have imagined Regan falling for—and a living reminder that, had her circumstances been different, she would never have chosen to get involved with a guy from the wrong side of the tracks.

Yet it was Connor she turned to in the night, not just willingly but eagerly. And when they came together, their passion was honest and real.

If that was all they ever had, he vowed it would be enough.

* * *

The next morning, as Connor made his way to the kitchen to start the coffee brewing, he found his brother in front of the mirror in the hall.

"You're up early today," he noted. "And all dressed up like a grown-up."

Deacon grinned into the mirror as he finished adjusting his tie. "What do you think?"

Connor, looking over his brother's shoulder, nodded. "I think you look like a lawyer."

"I'm a long way away from that, but I thought I should dress the part for my first day in court."

"I guess this is a pretty big opportunity, huh?"

"Huge," Deacon agreed. "And something else I owe to you."

"I didn't do anything except pass your résumé on to the sheriff, who gave it to his wife," Connor pointed out.

"That's the least of what you did," his brother said. "You always encouraged me to follow my dreams."

"I'm glad to see that you are."

"Actually, this is beyond my dreams." Deacon turned to face Connor now. "But you said that I could use the past to guide my future, but I should never let the past limit it."

"That sounds like pretty good advice," he said, lifting Baxter's leash off the hook by the door. "Here's some more—don't be late for your first day in court."

Deacon grinned in response to the not-so-subtle prompt. "I'm on my way."

When Connor and Baxter headed down Elderberry Lane, he saw a now-familiar red Toyota pulling into Bruce Ackerman's driveway.

"I haven't seen you around here in a while," he said,

when he caught up to Mallory as she was lifting her bucket of cleaning supplies out of the trunk.

She didn't look at him when she responded. "I picked up a couple more jobs, so my schedule isn't as regular as it used it be."

Baxter barked, as if to ask why she was ignoring him.

She turned to scratch his head, but dropped her chin so that her hair fell forward to curtain her face.

The deliberate motion set off Connor's radar. He took a step closer and tipped her chin up, the muscle in his jaw tightening as he noted the faded bluish-green bruise on her cheekbone. "What happened?"

She shrugged. "I ran into a fist."

At least her flippant response was honest. Of course, she had to know that he'd never believe that she ran into a door. They'd both heard that lie too many times, and he was furious and frustrated and sorry and sad for the sweet girl he'd known.

"Your husband's?" he guessed.

"Yeah, but it's really not a big deal," she said. "I mean, it doesn't happen very often. Usually, he treats me pretty good."

Connor shook his head. "Are you hearing yourself, Mallory? Do you realize how much you sound like your mother? Do you remember how much you hated the way she always made excuses for the men who knocked her around? The same excuses she made when she knocked you around?"

"Well, I guess it's true what they say about the apple not falling far from the tree," she said, though the color in her cheeks suggested that she was more ashamed of succumbing to the cycle of abuse than she wanted to admit. "But anyway, I'm fine."

"You mentioned a daughter."

"What about her?"

"Is she fine?" he wondered. "How do you think she feels when she sees her mother get knocked around?"

"He's never hit me in front of Chloe."

"Yet."

"Save the lecture for someone who needs it, Deputy," she advised.

"I'm not lecturing, I just—" he cut himself off, realizing that he was about to do exactly that. Because she'd heard it all before, and there was nothing to be gained by putting her on the defensive now. "Just promise that you'll call me if you ever need anything."

He handed her a card with his cell phone number on it; she tucked it into her pocket without even looking at it.

"Sure," she agreed.

But they both knew she was lying.

Chapter Seventeen

The day of the baptism dawned clear and bright.

The ceremony happened after the morning church service, by which time both Piper and Poppy were feeling a little restless and out of sorts. Everyone agreed the twins looked like perfect little angels in their matching christening gowns, but when it came time for the sprinkling with water, they screamed like little devils.

After the ritual had been completed, everyone gathered at the twins' grandparents' house on Miners' Pass. It was mostly a family event, although some of Regan's co-workers from Blake Mining and some of Connor's from the sheriff's office had been invited to attend. Holly Kowalski was there with her fiancé, and Regan was pleased to have the opportunity to thank her personally for the beautiful quilts she'd gifted to Piper and Poppy—and to offer her congratulations on the deputy's recent engagement.

"Why do I feel as if I've lost something?" Regan asked her husband, when Connor returned with the glass of punch she'd requested.

"Probably because you don't currently have a baby attached to your body," he noted.

"That might be it," she acknowledged, scanning the crowd for their daughters.

They'd been passed around from one person to the next all day and had held up pretty well—after they'd gotten back to the house and had their empty bellies filled. She located them quickly enough. Piper was in Auntie Brie's arms and Poppy was being cuddled by her cousin Dani, under the watchful eye of Auntie Kenzie. No doubt the little girl was going to be a great big sister when Spencer and Kenzie's baby was born.

"You were thirsty," Connor noted, when she quickly drained the contents of her glass. "Want a refill?"

She shook her head. "No, but I'm going to head inside to the powder room." She pitched her voice to a whisper, so that no one could overhear. "I have to adjust my nursing bra."

"Do you want me to come with you?" he whispered back. "I've got some experience with your undergarments."

"Taking them off," she acknowledged. "And that will have to wait until later."

"Promises, promises."

She was smiling as she walked into the house. And why not? She had a wonderful life and she was grateful for every bit of it. Okay, maybe not the bulky bra, she mused, as she adjusted the garment. But everything else was pretty darn good.

She exited the powder room and caught a snippet of conversation from the great room.

"—personally thank you for funding the Aim Higher Education Scholarship."

Regan stopped in her tracks.

She immediately recognized Deacon's voice—but who was he talking to?

"Blake Mining believes in giving back to the community."

Her father?

"Well, I'm grateful for that," her brother-in-law said now. "The funds have been of tremendous assistance."

Regan took a step back, her mind spinning.

She knew about Deacon's scholarship, of course, but she'd had no idea that the money had been put up by Blake Mining.

Was it a coincidence?

She didn't think so.

Especially when she recalled part of a conversation that she'd had with her husband several weeks earlier.

"...there was a weird message on my voice mail the other day from one of the junior accountants at work," she'd told him. *"...something about a scholarship fund."*

"He shouldn't be bothering you with trivial inquiries when you're on mat leave...let your father deal with it."

Had Connor known?

And if so, why hadn't he told her?

Determined to get answers to those questions from her husband right now, she pivoted quickly and nearly bumped into him.

"Hey." He caught her arms to steady her. "Are you all right?"

She nodded, then shook her head. But she didn't want to have a private conversation in the middle of the foyer, so she took his hand and pulled him into the library, closing the door behind them.

"If you wanted to be alone with me, you only had to say so," he teased, smiling as he moved in to kiss her.

She put a hand on his chest, halting his progress. "I heard your brother talking to my father."

His smile faded, his gaze shuttered. "Is that a problem?"

"That's what I'm trying to figure out," she admitted, as the hollow feeling in her stomach grew. "Did you know that Blake Mining paid for Deacon's scholarship?"

To his credit, Connor hesitated only briefly before nodding. "Yes, I knew."

Maybe he deserved some credit for being honest, but his truthfulness didn't lessen her feelings of betrayal. "And yet, I didn't."

"You've had more important things to think about over the past several months," he said reasonably.

She couldn't deny that was true, but she still had questions that she wanted answered. The most important one being: "When did you know about it?"

"Your dad mentioned the possibility of a scholarship to me shortly after Deacon headed to New York for his first term," he admitted.

"In the fall, then?"

He nodded again.

"Before or after you asked me to marry you?" she wanted to know. *Needed* to know.

Except that, in her heart, she suspected that she already knew. But she fervently hoped his response would prove her instincts wrong.

"Does it matter?" he asked.

"Of course it matters," she said. "And I'm guessing, from your deliberate effort to sidestep the question, the answer is before."

She read the truth—and maybe regret—in his gaze before he responded.

"Yes," he acknowledged quietly. "It was before."

Now she nodded, even as her heart sank impossibly deeper inside her chest. "How much?"

"How much what?" he asked warily.

Her eyes stung; her throat ached. "How much did it cost my father to buy me a husband?"

"It wasn't like that, Regan," he denied, reaching for her.

She stepped back, away from him. "Or maybe he was

more worried about the legitimacy of his grandchildren than his daughter's happiness?" she suggested as an alternative. Then she shook her head. "I can't believe I was such an idiot. That I actually believed you wanted to marry me and be a father to my babies, so they wouldn't grow up with unanswered questions about their paternity, like you did."

"I *did* want to marry you and I *am* their father," he said, sounding so earnest she wanted to believe him. "And even if you're upset that you didn't know about the scholarship, you have to know how much I love Piper and Poppy."

She nodded, because she did know. There was no denying that Connor loved their daughters. He'd also told her that he loved their life together, being a family.

But he didn't love *her*.

She hadn't expected happily-ever-after when they'd exchanged their vows. It wasn't part of their deal. Then again, she hadn't known he'd made a completely different deal with her father. And while they'd lived and worked together over the past eight and a half months—first preparing for the birth and then taking care of the twins— she'd been falling in love with him, and he'd been in it for the financial reward.

"You're right about the latter part," she acknowledged. "You are a wonderful father to Piper and Poppy. I just wish I'd known the real reasons you'd agreed to take on that role."

"I never lied to you, Regan." His tone was imploring, as if it really mattered to him that she believed him.

As if she could.

"Really? Is that how you justified the deception in your own mind? That you never actually lied?" she challenged. "Because you weren't completely honest with me, either."

"We each had our own reasons for wanting to get married," he reminded her. "And neither of us was under any illusions that it was for love."

"You're right again," she said.

"And everything I told you, all the reasons I gave for wanting to marry you, were true."

"But not the whole truth."

"You would never have agreed to marry me if you'd known the whole truth," he said.

"I guess we'll never know, will we?" she countered. "But one thing I do know is that I never would have assumed you were noble and honorable and—" She shook her head. "I was such an idiot. When I offered to pay for the kitchen renovation, you assured me you didn't marry me for my money. Because you married me for my father's money."

He flinched at the harshness of her words, but she refused to feel guilty for speaking the truth.

She swiped impatiently at the tears that spilled onto her cheeks. "If I'd known, I might still have married you," she decided. "I was so scared and desperate and alone, I might not have cared about your reasons. But at least then I would have gone into the marriage with my eyes wide open.

"And I wouldn't have been foolish enough to fall in love with you."

Before Connor could wrap his head around what she'd said, she was gone.

He was staring at the door through which she'd disappeared when her sister entered. "I came in to ask Regan where she put the diaper bag, and she walked right past without even seeing me," Brie remarked.

"Over there," he said, pointing to a chair in the corner.

His sister-in-law opened the top of the bag, took out a diaper and the package of wipes. "Why did she storm out of here?"

"Maybe you should ask your sister," Connor suggested.

"I'm asking you," she said.

He sighed wearily but knew there was no point in denying the truth. "I screwed up."

"Yeah, that was a given," she noted. "How badly?"

He just shook his head.

He should have ignored her father's directive and told her the truth in the beginning. But he'd been afraid that she'd say no and he really wanted her to say yes. Not just because he'd needed the money for Deacon's education, but because he'd wanted a chance to be with Regan. Of course, he never would have admitted that was a factor at the time, because he hadn't been willing to acknowledge his feelings for her.

"Regan can forgive a lot of faults," Brie said to him now. "But she can't tolerate dishonesty. She was involved with a guy once who had a pretty big secret, and when it was finally uncovered, she was devastated—by the deception even more than the truth."

He guessed that she was referring to Bo—the ex-colleague, ex-lover, with the secret family. And he realized that it didn't matter how he'd managed to justify, in his own mind, keeping the truth about the scholarship from Regan. She'd trusted him with her deepest secrets, and he hadn't done the same.

"I screwed up really, really badly," he confessed.

"Then you better come up with a really, really good

plan to fix it," she said. "Assuming you want to fix it because you're head over heels in love and can't imagine your life without her?"

"I am," he confirmed. He wasn't sure how or when it had happened, but he knew it was true.

"Then you might want to lead with that," Brie suggested.

When Connor got home, he found his brother in the living room with books spread out on the coffee table, a dog at his feet and a baseball game on TV. Deacon had left the party early to work on a pretrial memo that his boss had asked him to prepare, so he had no idea that his brief conversation with Regan's father had resulted in lasting fallout for his brother.

"Where's everyone else?" Deacon asked, noting that Connor was alone.

"They're staying at Miners' Pass tonight."

His brother hit the mute button on the TV to give Connor his full attention. "Why?"

"Because Regan's mad at me," he admitted.

"About?"

He shook his head. "It doesn't matter."

"Regan doesn't strike me as the type to go off in a tiff, so I'm guessing it was something that matters to her."

"Yeah." Connor scrubbed his hands over his face. "Maybe my mistake was in ever thinking we could make our marriage work."

Deacon frowned. "Why would you say something like that?"

"Because we're way too different."

"So?"

"So Regan's a Blake," he reminded his brother. "And that puts her way out of my league."

"Obviously Regan doesn't think so, or she would never have married you."

"She was pregnant and overwhelmed by the prospect of raising her babies alone."

"I don't have enough worldly experience to translate into words of wisdom," Deacon said. "So I'll suggest that you take your own advice."

"What advice is that?" he asked, a little warily.

"Let the past guide your future but don't let it put limits on it."

"I'm not sure that's really applicable to this situation."

"Well, it's all I've got," Deacon said. "Except to say that you owe it to yourself as much as Regan to fight for the family you've made together."

Regan was miserable.

She'd told Connor that she needed space and time to think about things, and he'd given it to her.

Idiot.

Why couldn't he know that what she really wanted was for him to fight for their marriage? To prove to her that she was worth fighting for. Or, if not her, at least Piper and Poppy.

Two days had passed since the party with no communication from him. On day three—Greta's day off—she responded to a knock on the door.

"Deacon, what are you doing here?"

"If the mountain won't come to Muhammad," he began.

She smiled at that. "Come in, Muhammad."

He stepped through the door and gave her a warm hug.

Inexplicably, her eyes filled with tears. Although she was mad at Connor and still feeling hurt and betrayed, she missed Deacon (and Baxter) and the rhythms and routines they'd established as a result of living together, and she really wanted to go home.

She'd only lived with her husband in the house on Larrea Drive for nine months, but it truly felt like home. And not only because Connor had renovated the kitchen in accordance with her preferences, but because being there with him—being his wife and a mother to their babies—she truly felt as if she was where she belonged. It didn't seem to matter why or how they'd connected, all that mattered was that they were a family together.

Without him, she felt alone and incomplete.

But she pushed that thought aside for now to focus on her visitor. "Can I get you something to drink?" she offered. "Soda? Coffee? Beer?"

"I'm not thirsty," Deacon said. "I just wanted to come by to make sure you were okay."

The unexpected overture and genuine concern in his expression caused her throat to tighten. "I'm fine," she said, though her tone was less certain than her words.

"And to ask how long you intend to punish my brother," he added.

"Is that what you think I'm doing?" she asked, startled by the question—and perhaps his insight.

"Isn't it?" he prompted gently.

Regan sighed. "I don't know. I mean, it wasn't a conscious decision, but maybe I did want him to feel some of the hurt I was feeling."

"He knows he screwed up," her brother-in-law said.

"I screwed up, too," she admitted.

Growing up a Blake in Haven—because despite her last name being Channing, everyone knew Regan was a Blake—everything had come easily to her. So much so that she'd taken a lot of things for granted. She hadn't delved too deeply into Connor's reasons for marrying her because she'd wanted a husband for herself and father for her babies, and she usually got what she wanted.

She was spoiled and entitled, and she'd proven it by running away when Connor didn't respond to the shouted declaration of her feelings with an equally emotional outburst. She'd wanted him to fight for their marriage, but why would he when she hadn't fought to stay with him?

"Well, for what it's worth, he's miserable," Deacon told her now.

"That makes two of us," she confided.

"So come home," he urged. "It will be more fun to watch him grovel up close."

She managed a laugh. "I'll think about it. Now, that's enough about your brother—tell me about your job."

"Katelyn's got a ton of cases on the go, so I'm working my butt off—and loving every minute of it."

"That's great," she said sincerely.

"We're doing jury selection in court tomorrow."

"That sounds like fun—unless you're in the jury pool."

He chuckled. "Yeah, most people grumble about getting the summons. But it really is a fascinating way to see the legal system at work."

They chatted a little bit more about his work, until Regan lifted a hand to stifle a yawn.

Deacon immediately rose to his feet. "That's my cue."

"It wasn't a cue," she protested. "I'm a new mom of twins—I'm always tired."

"Another reason to come home," her brother-in-law said, with a conspiratorial wink. "Make the dad do his fair share."

Chapter Eighteen

Connor was scowling at the coffeepot when Holly took the pot off the burner and filled a mug that she then pressed into his hands.

"You have to actually drink it for the caffeine to take effect," she told him.

He lifted the mug to his lips. "I didn't get much sleep last night."

"The twins keep you up?" she asked sympathetically.

He swallowed a mouthful of coffee. Missing the twins and their mother was what kept him up, though he didn't say as much. He didn't want anyone to know that his wife had left him because he was hoping it was a temporary situation soon to be rectified.

Regan had asked for time—but how much time was he supposed to give her? How much was enough and—

"Neal, Kowalski—you're with me," the sheriff said, striding briskly through the bullpen.

Connor put the mug down and automatically checked for his weapon and badge.

Holly did the same as she asked, "What's up?"

"Domestic," Reid said grimly.

"Damn," Connor muttered, falling into line behind his boss, who was already halfway out the door. "Who called it in?"

"Six-year-old kid hiding in the closet of her bedroom."

Connor swore again.

"It gets worse," Reid warned. "She claims her dad has a gun."

"Shotgun," Holly said.

Connor frowned as he reached for the passenger-door handle of the sheriff's SUV. "How do you know?"

"I don't." She nudged him aside with her hip. "I was claiming the front seat."

With a philosophical shrug, Connor moved to the rear door.

"Where are we going?" he asked, when the sheriff slid behind the wheel.

"Southside."

Connor's old neighborhood.

"Second Street."

He suddenly had a knot in his stomach the size of a fist. "Number?"

"Sixty-eight."

Mallory's house.

As the sheriff turned onto Second Street, Connor considered the possibility that the caller—the daughter Mallory had described as the light of her life—might be wrong about the gun. Sometimes kids had trouble separating fantasy from reality. And sometimes, he knew from personal experience, kids saw things that everyone else chose to ignore.

Either way, they were going to go in assuming the dad was armed—and hope like hell he didn't have more than one weapon.

Reid pulled the SUV over in front of number sixty-two so as not to tip off anyone inside number sixty-eight. He opened the back and handed out vests.

"The 911 operator said the kid was calling from her bedroom at the back of the house. Apparently there's a window accessible from the ground. Kowalski, go in and get the girl and let us know when she's safe.

"And no, I'm not keeping you out of harm's way," he said, before she could protest her assignment. "I'm sending you because the kid's terrified that her dad has a gun, so I don't want to send in another man with a gun."

Holly nodded. "Yes, sir."

"Neal, as soon as we get word that the kid's out of the house, you're going in the side door, I'm going in the front."

Though Haven was hardly a hotbed of criminal activity, bad things did occasionally happen in the town, and Connor had learned early on to trust his instincts when reading a situation. He was struggling to read this one. Although human nature was predictable, individuals often bucked the trends—especially when emotions were running high.

Evan Turcotte's emotions were running high, as evidenced by the pained expression on his face and the real tears in his eyes as he held his gun pointed at his wife. "You called the cops?" The gun shook in his hand. "How could you do that to me?"

"I didn't." Mallory's voice pleaded with him to believe her. "You know I didn't, Evan. I've been here with you the whole time."

Unable to argue with her logic, he shifted blame to the neighbors, using several choice adjectives to describe their interference in things that were none of their goddamned business.

"Do you have a daughter, Mr. Turcotte?" The sheriff spoke up now, attempting to engage the man and defuse the situation.

"Yeah," Turcotte admitted. "So what?"

"So maybe yelling at her mom and waving a gun around might have scared your little girl," Reid suggested.

Turcotte swore again and blinked hard, attempting to clear the moisture from his eyes. "Aww, man. Chloe called you?"

"She did," Reid confirmed. "Because she wants everyone to be safe."

"I've never laid a finger on Chloe," Turcotte said. "I wouldn't ever hurt my little girl."

"I'm sure it would be a lot easier for Chloe to believe that if you put the gun down," the sheriff continued in the same patient tone.

"Where is she?" Turcotte demanded. "Where's my daughter?"

"She's outside with Deputy Kowalski," Reid said.

"I want to see her."

"You put the gun down, and we'll make that happen," the sheriff promised.

"If I put this gun down, you're gonna put cuffs on me and haul me off to jail," Turcotte said. "I know how this works—I'm not an idiot."

"You're obviously upset about something, Mr. Turcotte. Why don't we talk about what that is?"

"I only want to talk to Mallory," he said, his voice filled with despair. "I want you guys to go so I can talk to my wife."

"If you know how this works, you know we can't do that," Reid said. "This is what's considered an active threat situation."

"It's okay, Sheriff," Mallory said, but the trembling of her voice suggested otherwise. "You should go so me and Evan can talk."

Connor stepped out of the shelter of the doorway, hoping the sight of a familiar face would reassure her. "We're not going anywhere."

She shook her head. "Please, Connor. This isn't—"

"Connor?" Turcotte's interjection sounded pained. "Oh, this is just perfect. My cheating wife—" his voice broke a little as he swung the gun from Mallory to the deputy "—and her lover."

"I'm afraid you've been given some misinformation," Connor said calmly.

Unfortunately, Mallory didn't exhibit the same coolness. She threw her arms up in the air. "Ohmygod— where do you come up with this stuff?"

"I found his card on your dresser and I know you're sleeping with somebody," Turcotte snapped at her.

It was obvious to Connor that the man was at the end of his rope—desperate to hang on to his family and unable to see that his actions were pushing them away. So he took another step forward, attempting to draw the man's attention back to him.

"If you want to be mad at someone, Evan, be mad at me." He deliberately used the man's first name and a friendly tone, attempting to establish a rapport. To encourage him to look for a peaceful resolution to whatever conflict had driven him to this point.

But Mallory's husband wasn't interested in rapport. "I've got enough mad—and enough bullets—to go around," he promised grimly.

"Come on now," Connor said, in the same placating tone. "Put the gun down so that we can talk."

"I don't wanna talk to you."

"Well, you don't want to be making threats—especially against an officer of the law."

"I'm done making threats," Turcotte said, and pulled the trigger.

* * *

Ben and Margaret hadn't said anything when Regan told them that she was going to be staying at Miners' Pass with her babies again. Or maybe her parents had said plenty—just none of it to her. And for the first couple of days, she was happy to avoid any kind of confrontation with them. She just needed some time to sort through her own emotions—the most prominent of which were hurt and anger.

Although she was furious with Connor, she suspected that the marriage idea hadn't originated with him. Not that she intended to let him off the hook on that technicality when he'd proven only too willing to go along with the plan, but right now, her attention was focused in another direction.

"This is a surprise," Ben said, glancing to his wife for confirmation when Regan walked into his office four days after the baptism.

"We didn't have a meeting scheduled," Margaret assured him.

"No," Regan agreed. "But I needed to talk to you and I didn't want to wait until dinner."

"Talk to *me*?" her father asked, his tone wary.

She nodded. "But it's good that you're both here."

"What can we do for you?" her mother asked.

"I'm trying to understand—" she broke off, mortified to discover that her eyes were filling with tears. *Again.*

"Regan?" Margaret prompted gently.

She tried to focus on her father through her tears. "I need to know—was it your idea or his?"

"I've only ever wanted what's best for you," Ben said.

"Yours then," she realized.

Margaret frowned and turned to her husband. "What was your idea?"

Regan's brows lifted. "Mom doesn't know?"

Her father sighed. "No one was supposed to know."

"Know what?" Margaret demanded.

Ben seemed to be struggling to find the words to tell his wife what he'd done, so Regan explained, "Dad paid Connor to marry me."

Margaret gasped. "Is it true?"

"No," he immediately denied. "I never gave Connor any money."

"Not directly," Regan acknowledged. "But you wrote a hefty check to his brother."

"The Aim Higher Scholarship," Margaret murmured, putting the pieces together.

Regan nodded.

"You can't seriously be upset that your father wanted to help your brother-in-law with his law school expenses," her mother chided.

"Except that Deacon wasn't my brother-in-law at the time and Dad didn't offer the money out of the goodness of his heart—he did it so Connor would marry me." She shifted her attention back to her father then. "But how did you know he'd go along with your plan?"

"I knew he'd put a mortgage on his house to pay Deacon's tuition," Ben confessed. "And I saw the way he looked at you, the day you told us you were pregnant, and I knew he'd do almost anything for you—even give his name to your babies."

There it was again, the reference to "your babies," as if her father knew—or at least suspected—that Connor wasn't their biological father.

"I don't understand," Regan said now. "For most of my life, you barely showed any interest in where I was or what I was doing, and now suddenly you're not only interested but interfering."

"We've always wanted what's best for you," Ben said again.

"Maybe you should have conferred with Mom first, because I don't think she believes Connor fits the bill."

"I'll admit I had some reservations when you first brought him home," Margaret said. "But only because he's not your usual type."

"What's my usual type?" Regan wondered.

"Well…" Her mother faltered a little. "You never really brought anyone home before."

"Or maybe you were just never there to meet the friends I did bring home."

"And if I had some reservations," Margaret continued, pointedly ignoring the truth of her daughter's remark, "well, the fact that you moved back home after only a few months proves they weren't unfounded."

"I didn't move," she denied. "I only needed some time to think about the fact that my husband had reasons for marrying me that I knew nothing about."

"How much time do you think you need?" her father asked. "Because you can't expect him to sit around waiting for you to stop being mad at him."

"I'm also mad at you," she pointed out.

"Do you want me to apologize?"

"Are you sorry?" she challenged.

"No," he admitted. "Because he's a good man—and a good husband to you and father to your babies."

She felt the sting of fresh tears. "He is a good husband and father."

"Do you love him?" her father asked gently.

She swiped at the tear that spilled onto her cheek. "Yes, but that doesn't make what you did okay."

"He loves you, too," he said. "Even if he hasn't told you so."

Another tear; another swipe. "How do you know?"

"Because your husband and I have more in common than you know."

"What do you have in common with Connor Neal?" Margaret asked.

Ben smiled at his wife. "For starters, we both fell in love with women who were way out of our league."

She smiled back. "It's true," she told their daughter now. "We've been together so long, I sometimes forget how socially awkward and financially challenged Benjamin was when we first met."

"That's your mother's way of saying I was a geek—and broke."

"But you were a cute broke geek," Margaret noted affectionately.

"And you were popular and beautiful and a Blake, and I fell head over heels the first time I saw you."

"And six months later, I finally agreed to go out with you—just so you'd stop asking," Margaret recalled fondly. "Then you kissed me good-night, and I was so glad I'd finally said yes."

Maybe it did warm Regan's heart to see the obvious and enduring affection between her parents, but she'd come into the office today to try to figure out what she was going to do about her own marriage.

"I need to go home," she suddenly realized.

"We'll see you at dinner then," Margaret responded, without looking away from her husband.

Regan shook her head. "No. I need to go home to Connor—to tell him that I want to make our marriage work."

"I think that's the right decision," Ben told her.

Before she could say anything else, her cell phone buzzed.

A quick glance at the screen revealed Connor's name on the display, and her heart skipped a beat.

"Are you going to answer it?" Margaret asked.

She nodded and swiped her finger across the screen. But when the call connected, it wasn't her husband on the other end of the line.

It was the sheriff.

"What's wrong?" Ben asked, when Regan disconnected.

She opened her mouth, then closed it again, unable to say the words.

"Regan?" her mother prompted, concern evident in her tone.

"He… Connor… He was shot."

"Shot?" Ben and Margaret echoed together.

Regan nodded. "He's okay," she told her parents, desperately clinging to that belief. "The sheriff said he was wearing a vest, but they took him to the hospital in Battle Mountain to be checked out, just as a precaution. I need to go there. To Battle Mountain."

"We'll all go," Margaret said.

Regan nodded again, but her feet remained glued to the floor while the upper part of her body seemed to be swaying.

"Sit down." Her mom nudged her into a chair. "I'm going to get you a glass of water."

Regan sat. She felt simultaneously hot and cold— empty inside and somehow full of churning emotions. But she didn't realize she was crying until her dad handed her a tissue as her mom returned with a glass of water.

"I wasn't done being mad at him," she said, dabbing at the wetness on her cheeks.

"So those are angry tears?" Margaret asked.

"I don't know why I'm crying," she admitted.

"Maybe they're tears of relief," Ben suggested. "Because you know he's okay."

"Maybe," she allowed.

"And maybe, somewhere deep beneath the hurt and anger, you're realizing that the phone call could have given you very different news," her dad said gently.

Fresh tears began to fall. "Ohmygod—he could have died."

"But he didn't," Margaret pointed out in a matter-of-fact tone. "And the sheriff said he's going to be fine."

But Regan knew she wouldn't believe it until she saw him for herself.

"I do love him," she sniffled.

"Then tell him that," Ben advised.

"I will," she vowed. "The first chance I get."

Connor didn't see why he needed to go to the hospital, but the sheriff had stood firm.

"You're going to get checked out," Reid insisted. "Then you're going to go home where your wife can fuss over your bruises."

Which didn't really sound so bad, except that Connor knew better than to count on Regan fussing over him. He was still trying to figure out how to convince her to come home.

"Knock knock."

He glanced over as the curtain was pulled back.

Mallory, a little girl he guessed was her six-year-old daughter, and another woman he vaguely recognized stepped into the exam area.

Though the effort made his chest hurt, he sat up on the table. "Hey," he said, not sure what else to say in the presence of the child.

"Hey," Mallory said back, and offered a wan smile. "You remember my sister Miranda?"

He nodded. "It's good to see you again."

"Same goes, Deputy," Miranda said.

"And this is my daughter, Chloe," Mallory said, brushing a hand over the little girl's hair.

"It's nice to meet you, Chloe."

The child watched him with wary eyes.

"The sheriff said you were okay," Mallory noted. "But we needed to see for ourselves."

"I'm okay," he confirmed.

Chloe didn't look convinced. "Daddy had a gun," she said quietly.

He nodded. "And you were very brave to call the police and tell them that."

"We learned about 911 at school," she said.

"Now you know why it's important to pay attention in class."

He caught the hint of a shy smile before she ducked her head again.

"Why don't we go see what they've got to eat in the cafeteria?" Miranda suggested to her niece.

"Mommy come, too," Chloe said, reluctant to let go of her mother's hand.

"You go with Aunt Mandy—I'll catch up with you in a few minutes," Mallory said, and pressed her lips to the top of her daughter's head.

"Promise?"

"Promise," Mallory said, and drew a cross over her heart with her finger.

The little girl finally let go of her mother's hand to take the one offered by her aunt.

"I'm glad you called your sister," Connor said.

Mallory nodded. "We're going to stay with her, here

in Battle Mountain, for a few days. We can't go home until the sheriff's department clears the scene, anyway."

"And then what?" he asked her.

She shrugged. "Hopefully I'll figure that out over the next few days."

"How's your husband?" When Turcotte pulled the trigger, the sheriff had responded—and Turcotte hadn't been wearing a vest.

"Still in surgery," she said.

"So…you finally told him you wanted a divorce?"

She nodded. "But I had no idea he had a gun. If I'd known…"

"If he makes it through the surgery, he'll be going to jail for a long time," Connor said, when her words faltered.

"I know." She brushed away the tears that spilled onto her cheeks. "I don't want him to die. He's the father of my child, but…I can't help thinking that she might be better off without a dad rather than have one who's in jail."

Her comment made Connor consider that never knowing his own father might not have been a detriment. It also reinforced his determination to be the best father he could be to Piper and Poppy—and any other kids he and Regan might have together, if he could convince her to give him a second chance.

Regan had planned to play it cool. For Connor's sake as much as her own. She understood that being a deputy wasn't just his job but an integral part of his identity, and she didn't want him to think she was going to get hysterical every time he had a little mishap on the job.

But this wasn't a minor mishap—this was a major event. Her husband had been face-to-face with an armed suspect, working to de-escalate a dangerous situation, and was rewarded with a bullet for his efforts. Someone had actually pointed a gun at him and pulled the trigger.

She couldn't envision the scene. She didn't want to. Every time she thought about Connor in that situation, she felt dizzy and nauseated and more terrified than she could ever remember feeling. But it was his job to put himself in exactly those types of situations and if she loved him—and she did!—she needed to accept that there were inherent risks to wearing a uniform and trust that he would take all necessary precautions to stay safe and come home to her and their daughters at the end of every shift.

Thankfully her parents had driven her to the hospital, so she didn't have to think about anything but Connor. Maybe they'd missed out on a lot when she was growing up, but they were here for her now and she was grateful for their support. She was also grateful that they opted to wait outside while she went in alone to see her husband.

Play it cool.

A reminder that she promptly forgot when she saw him sitting up on the examination table—alive and in one piece with no visible blood to be found. Unable to hold herself back, she flew into his arms.

He caught her close, enveloping her in the warmth and strength of his embrace. But she didn't miss the sharp hiss as he sucked in a breath.

She drew back, just far enough to see the pained expression on his face.

"What is it? What's wrong?"

"I'm a little sore," he admitted.

"The sheriff said that you were wearing a vest. That you weren't hurt."

"The Kevlar absorbed most of the impact," he conceded. "But a bullet still leaves a mark."

She pulled all the way out of his arms now to shove his T-shirt up, gasping when she saw the colorful bruise blooming in angry shades of red and purple against his skin. "Ohmygod."

"Are you going to kiss it better?" he asked.

"How can you make jokes about this?" she demanded, fighting to hold back a fresh onslaught of tears.

"It looks worse than it feels. Well, maybe not," he acknowledged. "But it's just a bruise."

"From a *bullet*," she said. "You could have been killed."

The devastating truth washed over her again, and she collapsed into sobs.

He tried to pull her back into his arms, but she held herself at a distance, explaining, "I don't want to hurt you."

"Having you here, being able to hold you, is the best possible medicine," he told her.

She wasn't sure she believed him, but she stopped resisting, because in his arms was where she wanted to be.

She sniffled. "I can't believe you were *shot*."

"It was pretty damn scary for me, too," he confided to her now. "And I did have a moment… My life didn't flash before my eyes…or maybe it did," he decided. "Because when I was staring at the gun, all I could think of was you.

"And I promised myself that if I made it out of there in one piece, I'd do whatever I had to do to make things right. Because you are my life. My everything."

He cradled her face in his hands, gently wiping the tears from her cheeks. "I love you, Regan. So much."

They were the words she'd wanted him to say, and hearing them now both filled and healed her heart.

"I love you, too," she told him.

He smiled then. "I kind of figured that out from what you said when you were yelling at me the other day."

"I was hurt and angry and—"

"And you had every right to be," he said. "I should have told you the truth from the beginning."

"Or at any other time over the past nine-and-a-half months," she suggested.

"You're right," he acknowledged. "But I was afraid that if I told you the truth, I'd lose you. And I didn't—don't ever—want to lose you."

"You're not going to lose me."

"Does that mean you'll come home?" he asked.

"I'd already decided to do just that when the sheriff called."

"Good," he said. "Because there's nothing I want more than a life with you and our daughters."

"I want that, too," she told him. "And…maybe another baby someday."

He brushed his lips over hers. "It's as if you read my mind."

Epilogue

"When my mom called to invite us for dinner, I didn't realize it was going to be a family affair," Regan remarked, as Connor pulled into the driveway where several other vehicles were already parked.

"Do you think they know it's our anniversary?" he asked.

"I wasn't sure *you* remembered it was our anniversary," she admitted.

"Of course I remembered. I even booked our suite at The Stagecoach Inn."

"*Our* suite?" she asked, amused.

"Well, I can't help but feel a little proprietary about the room where I first had the pleasure of making love with my beautiful wife," he confessed.

"I have very fond memories of that room, too," she assured him. "And I'm eager to make more, so what do you say we skip this dinner and go straight to the hotel?"

"An undeniably tempting offer," he said. "But unless you want to take Piper and Poppy with us, we have to go inside."

"But we don't have to stay for dessert."

He chuckled as he opened the back door to retrieve the babies' car seats. "We won't stay for dessert," he agreed.

But their plans for a quick meal and quicker exit were thwarted by the discovery that Father Douglas had been invited to share the meal—and preside over a renewal of Connor and Regan's vows.

"We weren't there to share in the celebration of your wedding," Margaret explained. "So we were hoping you would exchange vows again today."

"You might have asked if this was something we wanted to do, rather than springing it on us," Regan noted.

"I want to do it," Connor said, before his mother-in-law had a chance to respond.

"Really?" His wife sounded dubious.

Margaret clapped her hands together excitedly. "Oh, this is wonderful."

"I haven't said *I* want to do it," Regan pointed out.

"I'll let you two discuss," her mother said, and slipped out of the room.

"For what it's worth, I think my parents set this up to show that they've accepted you as part of the family," she said, when they were alone.

"I only ever cared that I was accepted by you," he told her.

"Then you don't want to do the vow renewal?" she asked.

"No, I do want to do it," he said again. "My only regret, when we got married, was that I couldn't be completely honest with you about the reasons for my proposal. So today—" he dropped to one knee on the marble tile "—I'm asking you to marry me again, to take me as your husband and a father to your children, with no secrets between us, knowing that I love you with my whole heart and will continue to do so for all the days of our life together."

"And I actually thought I was starting to regain control of my emotions," Regan said, as her eyes filled with tears.

"Is that a yes or a no?" Connor asked.

"That's a very emphatic yes," she told him. "Because I love you with my whole heart, et cetera."

He lifted a brow. "Did you really just say 'et cetera' in response to my heartfelt declaration?"

"*After* I said that I loved you," she pointed out.

He grinned. "In that case, let's go get hitched so we can get to part two of our honeymoon."

And that's what they did.

* * * * *

Don't miss Brielle's story,
the next installment in Brenda Harlen's miniseries
Match Made in Haven,
on sale August 2019.

And don't miss the previous books in the
Match Made in Haven series:

Claiming the Cowboy's Heart
Six Weeks to Catch a Cowboy
Her Seven-Day Fiancé
The Sheriff's Nine-Month Surprise

Available wherever
Harlequin Special Edition books and
ebooks are sold.

#2695 A FORTUNE'S TEXAS REUNION
The Fortunes of Texas: The Lost Fortunes • by Allison Leigh
Georgia Fortune is excited to travel to small-town Texas for a family reunion—until her car breaks down! Luckily, Sheriff Paxton Price comes to the rescue and they quickly realize the attraction between them is mutual! The only question is—can it last?

#2696 THE MAVERICK'S SUMMER SWEETHEART
Montana Mavericks • by Stacy Connelly
Gemma Chapman is on her honeymoon—alone! But when she befriends a little girl staying at the same hotel, Gemma suddenly finds herself spending lots of time with the girl's father: Hank, a rough-around-the-edges cowboy who might be able to give her the feeling of belonging she's always craved.

#2697 THE COWBOY'S SECRET FAMILY
Rocking Chair Rodeo • by Judy Duarte
Miranda Contreras is back and she has her daughter in tow. The daughter Matt Grimes didn't know about. But after fleeing a broken engagement, Miranda needs somewhere to go and her hometown is her best bet, even if it puts all her secrets in danger of coming to light!

#2698 IT STARTED WITH A PREGNANCY
Furever Yours • by Christy Jeffries
Animal rescue director Rebekah Taylor isn't a pet person—or the family type. But now she's pregnant and a newbie parent to an adventure-loving stray dog nobody can catch, kind of like Grant Whitaker, her baby's father. Except he's sticking around. Can Grant persuade Rebekah to trust in him?

#2699 HAVING THE SOLDIER'S BABY
The Parent Portal • by Tara Taylor Quinn
Emily and Winston Hannigan had a fairy-tale romance until he died for his country. So when Winston arrives on her doorstep very much alive after two years, Emily's overjoyed. Winston may have survived the unthinkable but he believes he doesn't deserve Emily—or their unborn child.

#2700 FOR THEIR CHILD'S SAKE
Return to Stonerock • by Jules Bennett
Two years ago, Sam Bailey lost the two people who mattered most. Now his daughter needs him. Despite their still-powerful attraction, Tara isn't ready to trust her estranged husband. But Sam is taking this chance to fight for their future, to redeem himself in Tara's eyes—so they can be a family again.

YOU CAN FIND MORE INFORMATION ON UPCOMING HARLEQUIN® TITLES, FREE EXCERPTS AND MORE AT WWW.HARLEQUIN.COM.

When Matt looked up, she offered him a shy smile. "Like I said, I'm sorry. I should have told you that you were a father."

"You've got that right."

"I've made mistakes, but Emily isn't one of them. She's a great kid. So for now, let's focus on her."

"All right." Matt uncrossed his arms and raked a hand through his hair. "But just for the record, I would've done anything in my power to take care of you and Emily."

"I know." And that was why she'd walked away from him. Matt would have stood up to her father, challenged his threat, only to be knocked to his knees—and worse.

No, leaving town and cutting all ties with Matt was the only thing she could've done to protect him.

As she stood in the room where their daughter was conceived, as she studied the only man she'd ever loved, the memories crept up on her…the old feelings, too.

When she was sixteen, there'd been something about the fun-loving nineteen-year-old cowboy that had drawn her attention. And whatever it was continued to tug at her now. But she shook it off. Too many years had passed; too many tears had been shed.

Besides, an unwed single mother who was expecting another man's baby wouldn't stand a chance with a champion bull rider who had his choice of pretty cowgirls. And she'd best not forget that.

"Aw, hell," Matt said, as he ran a hand through his hair again and blew out a weary sigh. "Maybe you did Emily a favor by leaving when you did. Who knows what kind of father I would have made back then. Or even now."

Don't miss
The Cowboy's Secret Family *by Judy Duarte,*
available June 2019 wherever
Harlequin® Special Edition books and ebooks are sold.

www.Harlequin.com